18 Sirk on Sirk

Sirk on Sirk

Interviews with Jon Halliday

The Viking Press
New York

The Cinema One series is published by
The Viking Press Inc., in association with
Sight and Sound and the Education Department
of the British Film Institute

Published in 1972 in a hardbound and paperbound
edition by
The Viking Press Inc.
625 Madison Avenue, New York,
N.Y. 10022

SBN 670–64715–2 (hardbound)
      670–01938–0 (paperbound)

Library of Congress catalog card number: 73–178855

Printed and bound in Great Britain

Contents

1644399

Cover: 'A sign: Malone, alone, hugging that goddamned oilwell, having nothing'. Dorothy Malone in *Written on the Wind.*

Presentation of Douglas Sirk

Who knows Douglas Sirk? It is not fanatical sectarianism to state the facts of the case and to protest vigorously against them: Douglas Sirk is the most neglected director in the whole of American cinema.... There is no serious study, no sign or festival to salute one of the most interesting and exciting personalities in the entire history of the cinema.[1]

Here, given that the interview below is largely self-explanatory, I would simply like to touch on a very few points: Sirk's cultural formation in Weimar Germany; an indication of the conditions under which he had to work in the cinema (conditions which defined extremely closely his freedom of action in both Germany and America); and a few of the many themes which run, usually just below the surface, through his works.

At the end of the First World War Sirk was eighteen. A few months later he was in Munich during the short-lived Bavarian Soviet Republic, the only revolution of the century largely dominated by poets and intellectuals. The Soviet (which until 1933 was customarily referred to simply as 'the German Revolution') was an experience which left its mark on everyone who lived through it.

The politics of revolution were paralleled by a culture of revolt. The immediate postwar years saw a flood of literature concerned with the revolt of the younger generation: an explosion from the start both highly confused and ambiguous. All attempts at political revolution between 1918 and 1923, in Berlin, Bavaria, Hamburg, Bremen, and elsewhere, were smashed. And, likewise, the revolutionary

Jack Palance as Attila in *Sign of the Pagan*

literary and dramatic explosion which followed on the war also broke up – to right and left.

Sirk started his career – as a theatre director – in a world dominated by these two factors: the experience of failed political revolution and a highly ambiguous cultural explosion, whose ambiguity was closely linked to the politics of the epoch, and yet was masked and often invisible for some time. This ambiguity was perhaps marginally accentuated by the influence of Freud's discoveries. Madness was increasingly acknowledged as a legitimate mode of coping with an impossible world, as was suicide (embodied in the genre known as *Schülerselbstmordromane*, or 'school-children's suicide novels').

Along with this went a re-efflorescence of a long-standing German interest in disease and illness. This was already apparent in a writer like Schnitzler, himself a doctor. But the product which best resumes this aspect of the age is Thomas Mann's novel, *The Magic Mountain* (1924). This is, of course, a many-layered work, but it embodies the idea that disease is more interesting than health. Sirk's interest in both individual and social disease, and breakdown – as moments of both drama and revelation – can be traced right through his cinema work from *Der Eingebildete Kranke* (1934) to *Imitation of Life* (1958).

Sirk's cultural formation as a theatre director is grounded deep in the classics.* This knowledge of the machinery of classic drama proved invaluable in the cinema, where Sirk was able to bend the apparently haphazard forms of the most recalcitrant Hollywood genres into a precise and powerful structure. Sirk was also a painter, and had studied the history of art. This carried over considerably into set-designing in the theatre and in his German films. And it also shows up in Sirk's control over lighting and composition. Even when produced under extreme time pressure, all Sirk's films show a painter's eye for light and space. Among the more sensitive critics who have appreciated Sirk's work (*Cahiers du Cinéma*, Andrew Sarris), it has tended to be this 'stylistic' aspect which has been given the most prominence. This is not wrong, inasmuch as 'style' means not only lighting and composition, but camerawork, music, and cutting—plus the ability to see a film in its entirety and continuity.[2] All Sirk's films (where he had freedom of action) show not only individual stylistic talents, but form integrated stylistic ensembles.

* See *Biofilmography.*

Precisely because a film is a composite product, the conditions of work need to be specified before any assessment of the role of a participant can be undertaken. This is particularly important in Sirk's case, since the ups and downs in his career are attributable to the conditions of production and not to oscillations in his own artistic vision.

It is striking that within the overall highly oppressive political context of Germany there was considerable freedom of manoeuvre on such matters as re-writing the script, lighting, camerawork, and casting. After little more than a year at Ufa, he was able to re-write *Schlussakkord* (1936) completely. In America things fluctuated greatly. Between 1942 and 1948 Sirk was under contract to Columbia, then in the grip of Harry Cohn. Since Cohn refused to let Sirk direct a film until 1947, Sirk's first five films were made as independent productions. On three of these (*Summer Storm, A Scandal in Paris*, and *Lured*) Sirk had control over the essentials – script, cast, camera, cutting – and they were projects of his own choosing, though made on very small budgets.

From 1950 onwards, Sirk worked at Universal. The studio did not interfere with his work, but his early period here was bleak: very small budgets and poor stories which were far from his own interests. Even after establishing his credentials many times over, Sirk could not persuade Universal to take on any of his own projects – until he met the maverick producer Albert Zugsmith, who was temporarily with Universal in the mid-fifties, and with whom he was able to make his best films, *Written on the Wind* and *The Tarnished Angels*.

Any appreciation of Sirk should start from his own projects, such as *Summer Storm* and *The Tarnished Angels*, since these allow one to see coherently what he was trying to do. Or compare *Imitation of Life* (Ross Hunter) and *Written on the Wind* (Zugsmith): both masterpieces but quite different types of film – a difference directly attributable to the producer. In *Imitation of Life* Sirk is fighting – and transcending – the universe of Fannie Hurst and Ross Hunter (not to mention Lana Turner, John Gavin, and Sandra Dee). In *Written on the Wind*, he is able to express more directly his vision of America.

'Style' and 'content' are thus less than ever inseparable in Sirk. Since Sirk's films are usually composites, they are also many-layered, and they have, therefore, to be read below their immediate surface.

Sirk himself in the interview strongly insists on the need to historicize the American melodrama. This is not simply because of the nature of the studio (the immediate conditions of production), but also because of the condition of society as a whole, at the time basking complacently under Eisenhower, while already disintegrating from within.

Two examples: *All that Heaven Allows* and *Imitation of Life*. On the surface, *Heaven* is a standard women's magazine weepie – mawkish, mindless, and reactionary. Yet just beneath the surface it is a tough attack on the moralism of petit bourgeois America. Within the story, and the genre (and the cast), Sirk has constructed a film which historicizes the lost American ideal of Thoreau and situates the barren ideology of bourgeois America in class terms. He does this by showing the *relations* between people whose roles are already specified – for example, at the country club, one of the most condensed scenes in all cinema. Relationships are also concretized in presents: Sirk's use of the festival of Christmas allows him to indicate in one sequence the oppression of the gift within the family in a diseased society (the presentation of the TV set to Jane Wyman).

Imitation of Life is another many-layered film. Here, more than in any other movie (except perhaps *Magnificent Obsession*), one can see Sirk's talents at work in adverse circumstances. The character played by Susan Kohner is promoted; and, admirably served by Russell Metty, Sirk has used his command over 'style' to transform the awful story more by light, composition, camerawork, and music than by anything else. It is not merely the gallery of show-business figures (agents, playwrights, actors, and actresses), but the lighting of the locales of show-business which is devastating: the office of Allen Loomis (Robert Alda), the night clubs where Susan Kohner works, for these are the sites of the imitation of life.

All these elements of 'style' are integral to Sirk's conception of the structure of films, itself integrally linked to the location of the genres *vis-à-vis* American history. Sirk refers to the precise distance writers like Euripides, Calderón, Shakespeare, and Lope de Vega had to take in presenting their critiques of their own societies within the established genres. His own position was very similar. Hence the interest of *Summer Storm* and *The Tarnished Angels*, both his own projects.

Summer Storm is based on Chekhov's novel *The Shooting Party*. Both the themes and the level of the critique in Chekhov's work are very close to those of Sirk. Chekhov, too, was working in a disintegrating society, a society of pretence and illusion, frequently befogged by alcohol. Yet he was writing for a relatively complacent bourgeoisie – with whom he has continued to be popular. *The Tarnished Angels* is based on William Faulkner's *Pylon*, set in the American South during the Depression. The Depression allows Sirk to go right to the heart of society, to catch it at its moment of breakdown. In conditions of poverty and scarcity, men and women are driven 'naturally' to extremes: to flying rickety planes, to parachuting, exposing oneself as an object of spectacle. The family has collapsed. The world has become such that the only escape is into the air. Even beds have lost their aura of security. 'How does Jack (her son) feel about beds?' Rock Hudson asks Dorothy Malone. 'Beds remind him of sickness.'

The America of the fifties, when Sirk was at Universal, was not *apparently* in a state of breakdown. *Written on the Wind*, too, is about decomposition, but in a society blind to its own condition. Since the accepted elements of the Depression are not available, Sirk piles on infirmity: alcohol, sexual frustration, fear of sterility, violence. From this point of view, one can consider *The Tarnished Angels* and *Written on the Wind* as complementary. Both are about breakdown, and failure.

Written on the Wind (a Zugsmith film) is the key to the Sirk–Ross Hunter cycle. In all these melodramas, Sirk is seeking the interstices of society, the chinks in its armour, the moments of both individual and collective breakdown. The doctor is a recurrent figure in Sirk's films. But in fact Sirk's approach is much broader than a purely medical one, since it encompasses the whole range of failure and doubt. There is a recurring use of doctors' consulting rooms, garish bars, and churches – the locales of breakdown. Sirk, of course, redoubles the implications of hopelessness by making religion, medicine, and alcohol ambiguous symbols. 'Convent and Hospital', says the sign at the opening of *Thunder on the Hill* (wherein the doctor is also a murderer); wine versus martinis in *All that Heaven Allows*. Sirk's bars exude cheerlessness and desperation: 'The principal problem is that the anaesthetics you get in these bars are never as good as the customer hopes' (Rock Hudson in *Magnificent Obsession*). The New England town in *All that Heaven Allows* is introduced from the church steeple, whence the camera pans down to the loneliness

11

and repression below. Paramatta, the prison in *Zu Neuen Ufern*, is likewise introduced via its church. Religion, like alcohol, is an escape, not a cure. Even doctors may not be able to provide this: 'Do you expect me to give you a prescription for life?' asks the doctor in *All that Heaven Allows*.

For Sirk is above all the artist of impossible America. His characters are trying to escape into the air, into bars, into churches. Others are simply attempting to mask their condition with pretence. People are often not what they seem to be. And, just as objects are recurrently promoted by Sirk to the same status as people, so people are frequently reduced to the consistency of shadows.

In a world of pretence, accentuated by the multiplication of intermediate objects (particularly mirrors and statues), Sirk's characters usually can find no way out. The possibility of change for the better is suggested in some of the earlier Universal films, but by the time of the Ross Hunter cycle, change is ruled out. So is successful suicide (death provides the resolution in four of Sirk's last five German films). It is this sense of entrapment, along with decay, which infuses much of the drama into Sirk's later American work. This is most explicit in *Written on the Wind*. With money proven an utterly worthless asset, alcohol of dubious assistance, and sexually frustrated, Dorothy Malone voices her final option: regression. 'How far we have come from the river.' But even regression, a theme hinted at in many of Sirk's films (children's silences, Reichian screams . . .) is blocked off. There is nothing left but to go on going round and round in a circle.

Sirk's own counterpoint to the condition of America is provided by his films of the 1950s set outside America. One can see *Taza, Son of Cochise, Captain Lightfoot*, and *A Time to Love and a Time to Die* even, as providing a breadth of possibilities unthinkable in contemporary America. *Lightfoot* is the most obvious opposite: a carefree, happy work *about revolution*, even though the hero is continually in the direst difficulties. Both *Taza* and *Time*, in spite of constant harassment from the US Cavalry and the Nazis, are love stories of a kind Sirk could never set in modern America. There is in all these films a sense of space and love and feeling quite distinct from the obsessive and frequently sick attachments of *Written on the Wind*, *Magnificent Obsession*, and others.

My strongest wish is that this book of interviews may provoke a re-viewing of Sirk's films. After that, I hope a proper critical study may emerge. There is much more to be said about Sirk's visual language and his uses of irony and structure. Such an enquiry could lead further into the problems of the cross-fertilization of film genres with elements from the traditional theatre: the relationships of drama, melodrama, and the cinema in general.

The conditions of the interview

When Mr Sirk gave me this interview, in the summer of 1970, he had not seen any of his films for over ten years. Many of them he had not seen for twenty, thirty, even thirty-five years. As will be seen, he has, therefore, talked about them mainly from a structural point of view.[3] He asked me to express his apologetic apprehension on this matter.

I for my part would like to thank Mr Sirk most warmly for giving so generously of his time, and for the care and thought put into the interview. I had a great time, and I hope something of my enjoyment comes across. If it, or Mr Sirk's intelligence and enthusiasm, should not transpire from the edited text, then the fault is entirely mine.

In conclusion, I should like to express my gratitude to both Mr and Mrs Sirk for their great kindness to me during my stay in Switzerland.

J. H.

NOTES

1. P. B. in Raymond Bellour and Jean-Jacques Brochier, eds., *Dictionnaire du Cinéma*, Editions Universitaires, Paris, 1966, p. 627.
2. On psychic continuity and the pleasure principle, see Thomas Elsaesser's remarkable essay on Minnelli in the *Brighton Film Review*, No. 15 and No. 18 (especially p. 12 of No. 15): Elsaesser's argument is equally applicable to Sirk.
3. 'I have a painter's memory. I can remember structures, not plots. I have tried to find order and rules in my pictures' (Sirk).

1: Germany: The Theatre

HALLIDAY: *There is rather conflicting evidence on your early life, so could we start with that? You are usually reported as having been born in Denmark. Did you go to Germany as a student and decide to stay there?*

SIRK: No, I didn't. I was born in Germany, in Hamburg. My father was Danish. He was a newspaperman, and at the time he was working for both German and Danish newspapers. I spent some years of my very early childhood in Denmark, and then my father returned to Germany to stay there for good, and became a German citizen.

So you didn't go to university in Copenhagen either, as is sometimes alleged?

No, I didn't. I went to the Universities of Munich, Jena and ultimately Hamburg.

What did you study? You are credited with all sorts of things in the sources.

I first studied law, but later on I gradually turned to philosophy and the history of art. And all the time I did some painting, which then was one of my main interests, and also some things to do with the theatre. But in between my time at the universities I did one year of newspaper work in Hamburg, partly in order to finance my studies. I worked on the same paper as my father had before he switched to being a school principal.[1] I still remember him introducing me to the editor of the newspaper. The building was situated on a square where the leading theatre in Hamburg – and in Germany – had been located, the one where the great Lessing had been *dramaturg*[2] and about which he wrote his *Hamburgische Dramaturgie*. His monument was right in the middle of the square and I still see my father pointing his wise finger towards the bronze effigy of Lessing and telling me, 'Boy, try to write like that man.'

You were in Munich during the Bavarian Soviet. What do you remember about that, and about people like Toller and Leviné?[3]

It was a nightmare, as confused and full of contradictions as a bad dream. First of all, we were all depressed by the war – and you must remember that the period just after the lost war was extremely tough on everyone. In Munich it was just hell. They were shooting in the streets, no one really knew what was going on, or where they were going to, and I think the Räterepublik didn't know either. The people round Toller were dilettantes, really. Then I didn't think so, being more or less one of the crowd, but later on it became clear to me that Toller especially was just a confused enthusiast as far as politics go. He was completely lacking in an understanding of the structure of the various political elements which formed that period. I knew Leviné slightly ... I met him a couple of times. He seemed the only person with the political competence to hold the thing together.

The one who then appeared to me to have the most interesting and profound approach to things was Landauer.[4] But he, too, was a man lacking in pragmatism. I met him a number of times, always wordlessly listening to him, and the influence of his thinking and of his personality has little waned in later years. But altogether it was a revolution without a real base among the masses: it was a revolution from above. Perhaps this was inevitable, since the Bavarian masses were then, as now, extremely conservative, and it may well have been impossible for a revolution to establish a base among them. At any rate, it collapsed, as you know. I think the only person with the political brain and the ability to have saved the revolution was Leviné. In a way, it is paralleled – but in reverse – by the July 1944

15

affair, which was also an attempt at change from above, without any mass base.

Anyway, as a whole it was a nightmare, and ultimately I was glad to get out of Munich, just before the final collapse, and continue my studies at Jena, and then Hamburg. When I got to Hamburg I sat down to write a play on the whole business, which I wanted to call something like *Deep Above* (*Unten Oben*). I don't think it was a good play: I was still too near to the events. Later I offered it to Dr Eger, the head of the theatre where I was working: he thought it was crazy, like I was.

So it was in Hamburg that you started out in the theatre?

Yes. Again, as during my newspaper period, it was first a job to finance my studies, because I was still at the university. It was in Hamburg, too, that I had my first encounter with Einstein's theory of relativity. I heard him speak at the university there. Of course, I didn't grasp it entirely, but I was moved somehow by the dark and mighty breath of the new century which in almost every respect had begun in those early twenties.

Another influence on me was Erwin Panofsky,[5] later the great art historian, under whom I studied. I was one of the select in his seminar, and for him I wrote a large essay on the relations between medieval German painting and the miracle plays. I owe Panofsky a lot.

And it was while I was still studying the history of art that I became a second-line *dramaturg* at the Deutsches Schauspielhaus in Hamburg, one of the biggest and best theatres in Germany. I earned very little money, because the post of second *dramaturg* was considered the most superfluous thing in the theatre....

At any rate, I got sick and tired of just recommending plays which were not being done, so I went to Dr Eger – who later on became a very good friend of mine and head of the German Theatre in Prague – and told him I wanted to stage a play. This was in 1922, I think. So he told me I was mad. But the gods, being always in favour of madness, were on my side. They let a director fall sick, and the theatre had to come out with a new play, *Bahnmeister Tod* (*Stationmaster Death*) by a young playwright, Bossdorf by name.[6] He died a few years later. There was no one else interested in doing

16

this rather odd piece of drama, so it was handed to me and I staged it. It was not at all my kind of play. But it was a chance, especially being that young, and in a very big theatre, and I had first-rate actors. To my surprise – and everyone else's – it turned out to be a big success, particularly among the critics. From there on I was lost to the theatre.

So Dr Eger said he would raise my salary, and every now and then he'd also let me stage a play, 'one of those crazy modern plays', he said, meaning Expressionism. But, being youthfully conceited, I told him I wanted to do the classics, Shakespeare mainly. He told me I didn't have the experience, or the wisdom, or the understanding, or what do I know. So I left, and went to Chemnitz.

Because there, on account of my recent directorial success, I had been offered a completely independent post as *Oberspielleiter*, or first director – and this was something I couldn't resist. I started with Molière, Büchner, and Strindberg. And, sure enough, the theatre went broke, right at the beginning of the season – this was 1922–23. It was a privately-run theatre, and the money man and manager of the theatre gave up and vanished overnight. But naturally, we, actors and technicians, had to go on. So a collective was formed and they elected me head of the theatre. This was my first experience with a collective, and not a very encouraging one. There was a majority of young actors, all of them enthusiasts, but at the same time, in order to survive, the box office was important. So pretty soon it was just comedies, comedies and melodramas: things that made money. Among other plays I did *Madame X* there, which many many years later came back to me as a movie script, staring into my face, awakening unpleasant memories.

At any rate I gained experience there, learned my craft. And I also learned to handle actors under the *most* strained circumstances. . . . You mustn't forget that it was the time of the inflation. The takings were tiny, and we used to distribute them all among the collective and then just before midday you ran to the bank, because the banks pulled down their shutters between 12 and 2 o'clock before the new dollar rate went up at noon. And if you got in too late you had just a small percentage left of what you had earned. . . . It was a pretty terrible time. And then from there I went to Bremen, to a much better theatre and a more sophisticated town, to take up the same position, that of *Oberspielleiter*.

But you never thought of going into the movies at this point?

I did just work once in the movies, in 1923. When I was moving my job from Chemnitz to Bremen I stopped off in Berlin, I went to visit a studio, and a movie director whose name I've forgotten gave me a job in the set-designing department. I took it over the summer because I needed to earn some money. It was just a temporary job, and then I had to go on to Bremen.

Were you still painting after you went into the theatre? Did you keep this up?

Yes, in a way. As a matter of fact, for some time I didn't know whether I wanted to be a painter, a theatre man, or a writer. Because as a young man I dabbled in rather a lot of things. I did a translation of Shakespeare's sonnets, for example, which was published in about 1922, with some illustrations by one of the Brücke painters, Joseph Eberz.[7] I also translated several of Shakespeare's plays,[8] as well as doing some writing of my own. But the painting I did from now (1923) on was mainly sets, and sketches for the plays I was staging – and later the pictures.

There is a book which deals with your work at Bremen,[9] but it is hard to see from it what your theatrical style was. How did you manoeuvre between all the various currents at the time, when Expressionism must still have been dominant in the German theatre?

Well, don't forget that I belong to a generation which was trying to get out of Expressionism already: from my very first days as a director I was not really Expressionistic, even in Chemnitz – while all around me Expressionism still bloomed, you know. This is why I later on came to like Bronnen and Brecht. Bronnen's play, *Vatermord* (*Parricide*) had quite an impact on my whole generation, I guess. I didn't recognize then, as I did later, that this play, as well as Brecht's first plays like *Im Dickicht der Städte* (*In the Jungle of Cities*) and *Baal* still had the marks of Expressionism. Brecht was trying to free himself from the style, but he was still under its influence, and he only managed to turn away from it when he embraced marxism, and this philosophy gave him his new style. I think

18

marxism in his artistic development is just as much an aesthetic necessity as a political one.

In Bremen, though, my set-designer, Lamey, with whom I worked for a very long time, and who was a good guy to work with, was still an Expressionist, in a way. He was a very young man. And a good painter. Of course, his sketches and designs for my plays as you see them in the book never were quite realized like that. I changed most of them: they were a taking-off base for what we had in mind or was dictated by circumstances. Most of the time we had to sit up half the night painting sets. Bremen was not a very big town, and the Bremen Schauspielhaus, like the theatre at Chemnitz, was not in any way financed by the town: it had to stand on its own feet. And it was a repertory theatre, with a constantly changing programme – and you needed a lot of stuff to survive. You put on a play, it ran for a couple of weeks, and that was that. If you had a flop, this was a disaster – and most of the really good plays were, commercially speaking, not too hot. For example, I staged Strindberg's *Dream Play* – this was one of the very few times it was put on in Germany, and it ran only for a couple of days, although it was an excellent performance, way ahead of its time, I think; and even the critical applause was unanimous. But the public was still too conservative not to be bewildered.

The Schauspielhaus at Bremen was owned by two men, Dr Ichon and Mr Wiegand. It was rather an unusual venture. But they were both mad about the theatre, and both decent men. Understandably, they tended to frown, benevolently, on anything that didn't promise to become a commercial success, and I couldn't go too far. Still, during my time the theatre achieved an excellent reputation as probably the best privately owned stage in Germany. As much as possible I was trying to combine commercialism with highbrow stuff like the classics: as you can see from the book, I did a lot of classics in Bremen, in a strictly commercial theatre. It was not easy to put over, say, *Antony and Cleopatra*,[10] or *Cymbeline*. Both of them earned critical acclaim, but little money – even *Cymbeline*, to my chagrin, which was then one of my favourites, a work of Shakespeare's late, manneristic period; and the temptation was to try finding a style for it. Now, you can imagine, speaking about style, how far that already is, must be, from Expressionism, because it was the ornate style of the masks, of the post-Elizabethan theatre. A style of ambiguity. But otherwise my staging of Shakespeare in Bremen was rather directed

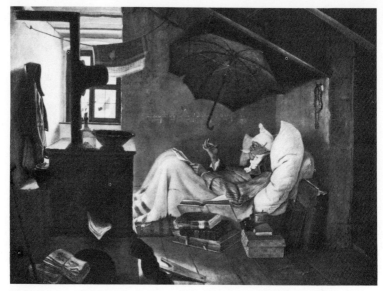

The influence of painting: Karl Spitzweg's painting, *Der Arme Poet* (The Poor Poet), and (opposite) the poet Knips (Alfred Abel) in Sirk's *Das Hofkonzert*

towards absolute simplicity, towards the minimum of décor – this goes mainly for the early and middle period of Shakespeare's work.

I notice you staged Bronnen's Rheinische Rebellen: *this was written at the time of the French occupation of the Ruhr, wasn't it? Can you understand what happened to somebody like Bronnen, because he is one of the most extraordinary figures in German culture: first a marxist, then a Nazi, and finally ending up in East Germany?*

Well, I have a kind of an explanation, perhaps. This is a very large and enormously complex subject, but I would like to try and say something about it, just briefly. I happened to know Bronnen rather well. He came down to Bremen to see *Rheinische Rebellen*, and was most enthusiastic about it. I spent a couple of days with him. I found him a very handsome, pleasant, most intelligent, and arrogant man. And already then I sensed something, I couldn't call it Nazism, it was too early for that, but let me call it a kind of rightism. And you do

20

feel it in his play, too. I was very surprised that he was still such a very close friend of Brecht, who then was definitely turning to marxism. You know this pair were known as the two *Dioscuri* of the German theatre at the time.

But you must remember that the period after the First World War was a time of great cultural upheaval: there were lots of things in the air, and it was often very hard at the time to know quite how to assess them politically. Everyone's thinking was political: when we came out of a movie or a play, or had read a novel, I and my friends, who were more or less left-wing at the time, would ask each other: where do you think he stands? – meaning the author of the play or the novel.

But later on in Leipzig, when I went to be the head of the Altes Theater there, I inherited from my predecessor, Dr Kronacher, another play by Bronnen called *Reparationen* (*Reparations*), which already had a disgusting and definitely extreme nationalistic connotation to it, to say the least. And for that reason I tried to get it scrapped – but the theatre was tied by a contract, and it had to go on.

A sketch by Richard Lamey for Sirk's stage production of Schiller's *The Robbers*

Bronnen appeared himself, and I had quite an unpleasant time with him. He didn't like my attitude towards his play, nor the fact that I didn't want to stage it myself and had given it to one of my directors. I sensed then that the Bronnen of the Brecht–Bronnen line had taken a complete turn towards Nazism, which proved to be true. Apart from that, *Reparationen* was pretty lousy as a play: it was undramatic – just a pamphlet in dialogue.

Bronnen was one of the many people caught in the awful contradictions of German culture and society, since he was half Jewish, and I think he tried to escape from his Jewishness by throwing himself into the arms of the Nazis. How was this possible? He explained that he was the illegitimate son of his non-Jewish mother, and he got her to affirm this – something that made me hate him even more. Although it was then not an unusual practice for certain people standing in between the races.[11]

One of the other things that emerged from the book on the Bremen theatre is a brief comparison of your staging of Schiller's The

Robbers *with that by Piscator*[12] *in Berlin at the same time. Is this something you can discuss: can you recall your production – and did you see Piscator's?*

I never saw Piscator's staging. I wasn't in Berlin then, so I can't compare it with mine. All I know is that my staging was based on a then rather extreme idea: I made the robbers into students who have run away from university, almost like you might do it today if you wanted to bring it up to date. I re-read the reviews in the book, too, and I was amazed how modern my production must have been.

You put on the Dreigroschenoper: *how did that go down in Bremen?*

It was a tremendous success, surprisingly enough, because Bremen was, in a way, a very conservative city. It was even a little bit of a scandal, too. People booed and hissed, and even left the theatre. And the managing directors, Ichon and Wiegand, were kind of timid at first; they didn't want to go on with the play, because they were afraid of losing their audiences. But perhaps the scandal helped, and anyway it turned out to be a very big success.

I played it *extremely* harsh – more so, I think, than Brecht had intended. Brecht had planned it more or less as a piece with music. Weill's music, though, was most aggressive (and this is an example of the impact he had on Brecht as well as on our entire generation). Later on, maybe six months later, when I was in Berlin, I saw the performance there. It was indeed different. I talked to Brecht about my conception, and he said, 'By all means. It's good to have variety.'

I had another experience with the play. As you know, it was made into a picture by Pabst, the great movie director. Pabst, I think, had been to see various performances of the play, and among these was mine. He talked to me about his picture. Later on, when I was in Berlin – it must have been the time when he was already having trouble with Brecht – he took me round, showed me the sketches for the picture, and took me to the Ufa studio where he was planning to shoot it. There was a huge model of old London, one of the most impressive things production-wise I have ever seen. We talked at some length about the whole thing. Unfortunately, I never saw his picture, and couldn't tell you how good it was – as you remember, it

Cartoon from the Bremen (*Volkszeitung*) of characters in Sirk's production of *The Threepenny Opera*. Hilde Jary (Mrs Sirk) is third from left

was disowned by Brecht. But Pabst was a great director, someone I admired very much.

There is one very perplexing illustration in the book on the Bremen theatre: a photograph of your production of Othello *in eighteenth-century dress – how come?*

That is because the prose translation of Shakespeare which I was using – which was the first translation into German – was done in the eighteenth century, by Eschenburg. The point is that this translation of *Othello* is so rooted in its time by the mere fact of language that it has become an eighteenth-century play, and so I staged it that way, like a Beaumarchais play.

I also read that you acted in a few plays at Bremen: is that right?

I only acted a few times. I had to do so several times in my own productions when someone fell sick. And at Chemnitz I acted in a number of funny roles, which are better forgotten. My best part, though, was in Strindberg's *Easter*. I do remember also acting in *Medea* by Grillparzer, at Bremen. At least I acquired some acting experience, let's say, but I never was a good actor, and as quickly as possible I stopped.

And from Bremen you went to Leipzig?

That's right. I went as the director of the Altes Theater, which was a very beautiful old rococo theatre, a playhouse where the young Goethe used to sit as a student and watch plays. Leipzig at the time was known as the little Paris: a very lively city, with one of the most famous universities on the continent. But the moment I came there it was not a very pleasant place. The great Depression started – this was the winter of 1929–30, a very tough time for the theatre, as for all the arts. Most Germans were out of work, and when the theatre opened at night there were hundreds of people there begging for a dime, for a groschen, for something, because they were out of work, and a whole segment of the population just couldn't afford to go to the theatre any more. Only the more expensive seats used to be filled; the upper ranks stared down at you in ghostly fashion – empty.

I haven't been able to find much information on your Leipzig period: can you tell me about your work there?

Certainly. And there are one or two plays I put on there I would like to say something about. As I told you, this was the time of the Depression, as well as of the sudden rise of Nazism, and some people like Bronnen and Johst [13] had already swung well to the right. It was already a fairly tough time – though I didn't realize then how much tougher it would get, so one of the first plays I put on there in Leipzig was a rather leftish piece called *Im Namen des Volkes!* (*In the Name of the People*) by Bernhard Blume. This was a play about Sacco and Vanzetti – and a rather good one. I put it on early in 1930, and it caused quite an uproar. In other parts of Germany it was banned, in the areas where the Nazis already held power locally, or swung a certain amount of weight. Leipzig, to a degree, was still free of that. Later on, when Hitler came to power, this was one of the plays which was, naturally, dragged up against me constantly. Still, I have a good memory of it, and a good production of mine it was, too, I think.

It was a very unsettling time. People were anxious and uneasy, and not yet entirely committed to the Nazi creed. For instance, I remember when I was staging Schiller's *Don Carlos* in the Altes Theater, there is a line where the Marquis Posa says to King Philip: 'Sire, give freedom of thought' – just that, but people started clapping like mad. I had seen the play quite a few times before, and this line had never made any special impression. But now, evening after evening, a large part of the audience started clapping. People still wanted to show how they felt then. Pretty soon they weren't given any chance any more. Though I, for one, never expected the Nazis to make it.

Can you tell me what it was like when the Nazis came into power? What happened in the theatre? Did conditions change a great deal?

I naturally could tell you a lot, stories upon stories. But it is impossible to go into it at length: it is really too vast a subject, too complex. It was a horrible period, exciting in a nerve-wracking way – and very tough on a man like me, who was responsible for a theatre, and everyone who worked there. To my right and to my left people were being chased away from their posts. I survived, and for one reason only. The mayor of Leipzig at the time was a man who was very close to Hitler, though not a Nazi, a man who has become part of history. This was Dr Goerdeler, later on executed by the Nazis for his part in the July 1944 plot – which, as you know, was the only significant opposition to the Nazi regime. Goerdeler, like the group around him, was an old-fashioned conservative democrat, and a close friend of Hugenberg's.[14] He later became a cabinet minister of Hitler's, as a representative of the Hugenberg group. Basically, he was an honest, highly educated German of the old school, a kind of Adenauer. He came from Koenigsberg, the city of Kant, and he was a Kantian himself, with the same unshakable ethical beliefs, the moral stubbornness, though his mind had not been sharpened by any experience of marxism, whether accepted or rejected. And then after the 1944 plot, as you know, he – like almost all of the others in his group – was executed. They hung this Kantian man on a meat-hook, like an animal, letting him die this way. Later on, after hearing about this, it has followed me as a constant nightmare and has hardened me towards any kind of totalitarianism.

At any rate, thanks to Dr Goerdeler I kind of survived in my post. But it was not a comfortable survival. The Nazis were telling you what to do, and what to stage. You couldn't do this, and you couldn't do that. . . . For instance, you couldn't stage Shaw any more because he was supposed to be a Jew, or Wilde, because he was homosexual. And each day I would find an article in the papers attacking me for having put on this or that play because it had something to do with issues that were hateful to the Nazis.

And, in addition to that, it was a time of great disloyalty. I had brought a number of actors with me from Bremen, whom I cherished as my friends, as of the same cut of mind as mine. They had often told me they were thankful to me for their entire careers. And overnight some of them turned out to be Nazis, and started doing everything they could to alibi themselves by disowning me, by cutting any bonds of friendship there had been between us. I fairly soon was a pretty lonely man there in my director's office. . . . The whole thing made me look at people with great care. It made me doubtful about people . . . a pessimist. And this saddened me greatly.

At the beginning the situation wasn't absolutely hopeless. It was a bit like Czechoslovakia five weeks after the Russian invasion. It took time, and then even when it became absolutely unbearable running a theatre, dealing with the countless interferences, it was still not too bad in the movies, because the foremost German company, Ufa, was privately owned by the Hugenberg group. And this was partly the reason why I decided to shift to the cinema, in 1934, while I still remained in charge of the Leipzig theatre, because Goerdeler insisted on that.[15]

Now, to go back to 1933, I would like to tell you about one play I put on, a very good play indeed, which got me into a lot of trouble – and that was *The Silver Lake* (*Der Silbersee*) by Kaiser [16] and Weill, both known as leftish people, in addition to which Weill was Jewish. I was getting this ready in January 1933 when the Nazis came to power. It was a play of tough social criticism, ten times tougher than any Brecht play. It is all about hunger and poverty. Weill had written some really powerful songs which I think are among the best things he ever did. Caspar Neher, Brecht's set-designer, had fashioned the sets. And Brecher, who had conducted Weill's original *Mahagonny*, which had opened in Leipzig in 1930, was leading the orchestra. The play was scheduled to have its opening night at the Leipzig theatre on February 18th, and then to open in Berlin the following evening.

Well, the Nazis came into power, and one of their town councillors, a man called Hauptmann – who wasn't one of the worst of them – asked me to drop the play. Otherwise, he told me, something would happen. So I got together with Kaiser, Weill, and Neher, since it concerned them personally as well, but we decided to go ahead, feeling the play to be artistically as well as politically very important. On the morning of the opening Dr Goerdeler called me up and advised me it would be best for me to fall ill and postpone the opening for a couple of weeks, and then everything could be let quietly drop. So I told him that I thought it was a time when it would be disastrous not to stand by one's opinion and give in. He then told me that he had information that the SA and the Nazi Party would block the opening, and he would seriously advise me to call the whole thing off. I said I wouldn't. Only two people can call off the play, I told him – he, as the mayor of Leipzig, or I, as the sole person responsible for the Altes Theater. He answered that if things went badly he might not be able to cover me.

But I went ahead, and the play was a huge success. The SA filled a fairly large part of the theatre and barracked away, and there was a vast crowd of Nazi Party people outside with banners and God knows what, yelling and all the rest of it. But the majority of the public loved the play, in spite of all the racket the Nazis made. You see, this was at the beginning of their rule.

Did you keep it on after that?

Yes, I did. I ran it for about thirty or thirty-two performances, all completely sold out, and we had the SA in there every night barracking and rampaging around.

What happened to the Berlin opening?

They scrapped it right after the experience of my première.

Weren't you harassed after something like that?

Yes, I was. There was a very bitter attack on me in the Nazi Party paper, the *Völkischer Beobachter*.[17] And then, I think right after the first night, Weill and Brecher fled. I still think it was a good production, and probably my most mature effort in the theatre – a kind of milestone in theatrical history ... or rather the end of a chapter. Hans Rothe, the famous translator of Shakespeare, later wrote that this was the occasion when the curtain rang down on the German stage.[18]

In a strange way, though, this also contributed to the way I felt about the Nazis. They did make a lot of trouble. They turned up and staged scandals. But you could go ahead with a play, and the audience was still such that they couldn't stop it being a success. And so I thought at first, well, things are going to be tough but perhaps it isn't impossible to overcome. Of course, things turned out to be not like that at all. No play, no song could stop this gruesome trend towards inhumanity.

There is also a reference to you having been supposed to become the head of the Berliner Staatstheater just before the Nazis came in: is that right?

Yes, that is correct. A few weeks before Hitler got into power I had almost concluded a deal, which only needed the approval of the Prussian State officials, and signatures. The Staatstheater used to be a huge theatre with two parts, a house for opera and a house for drama, and I was going to be the head of the drama part. But then the Nazis suddenly came into power. The administrative head of the whole thing told me, 'My dear friend, you must realize it's out of the question for you to take over the theatre since, I'm sorry to say, you have a Jewish wife.'

You are also credited with being involved in the Heidelberg Festspiele in 1935: is this correct?

Yes, it is. Let me tell you about that. I got an invitation, very much to my surprise, given my political reputation, to put on two plays at this festival: a play by Kleist, *The Broken Jug* (*Der Zerbrochene Krug*), and a medieval play called *Lanzelot und Sanderein*. Then the man in charge of the festival, Mr Laubinger, who was an important

Nazi,[19] had a heart attack in the middle of the preparations for the event. When I woke up next morning there was a telegram telling me I was in charge of the whole festival. It turned out a nightmare for me. There was Mr Hitler, Mr Goering, Dr Goebbels, what do you know.

Kleist was having a big revival in Germany at the time, so he was a safe bet, wasn't he?

That's right, he was. I've always distrusted the right-wing fellows, but there are some exceptions, like Kleist, who certainly belongs to the pantheon of German literature.

Anyway, the Heidelberg experience left a very bitter taste on my tongue, and I realized I had to do something to get out of the whole awful German nightmare. Now, at that time I couldn't, because I had had my passport taken away by the Nazis, so I was stuck.

How did that happen?

I'd been trying to arrange a job in Czechoslovakia, with my friend Dr Eger. Leipzig is very near the Czech frontier, and I'd been motoring down in between plays to organize a group of German-language theatres there, the Städtebundtheater. Anyway, someone told the police I was smuggling money out of the country, and so, after a number of interrogations, they removed my passport.

You are credited with a play entitled Regen und Wind: *did you write this?*

Well, yes, I did write it, in a way. It was based on an English play by a man called Merton Hodge, *The Wind and the Rain* – the title being taken from the fool's song in *Twelfth Night*, you know.[20] A German publisher asked me if I would translate the play and adapt it – because it needed adapting. It is so definitely Scottish: people in Germany wouldn't have understood it. It turned out to be rather successful. It opened first at the Kammerspiele in Munich, and then it went on at the Reinhardt Theatre in Berlin. I saw the performance there, which took place right at the beginning of the Hitler regime, I think. After that it went on in about fifty towns in Germany, and did very well.

Was Max Reinhardt a stage director who interested you much?

Well, he was the biggest director in Germany before the Nazis, but my own style was completely the opposite of his, right from the start.

How about Meyerhold: did you go and see his productions when he came to Germany?

Yes, indeed I did, and I met him when he was in Berlin. A man full of genius; but his work was functional and kind of expressionistic, I found. I saw his staging of an operetta, *Giroflé Girofla* – which was nothing like an operetta any more, of course.

NOTES

1. The *Neue Hamburger Zeitung*.
2. Roughly: 'play reader and adapter'.
3. The Bavarian Soviet Republic was a short-lived revolutionary government centred on Munich in April 1919. It followed on from a republican government which had been in power since November 1918, which is usually referred to in German as the Räterepublik (lit. 'Council Republic'), the term Sirk uses, which can also cover the whole period from November 1918 until the first days of May 1919 when the Soviet regime was brought down. Ernst Toller, subsequently a famous poet and playwright, was one of the leading members of the Soviet Republic (his experiences are described in his vivid autobiography *I Was a German*, London, 1934). Toller was given five years' imprisonment after the fall of the Soviet. He committed suicide in New York in 1939, shortly after the fall of Madrid. Eugen Leviné was a Communist who headed the second Soviet government in Munich (against Communist party advice). He was captured by the German (White) Army, and executed on 5 June 1919, aged thirty-six.
4. Gustav Landauer, who had translated Walt Whitman into German and was an acknowledged authority on Shakespeare, was commissar for culture in the Soviet government. When the Whites occupied Munich he was kicked and beaten to death by White officers. Before he died, he told the soldiers, 'I have not betrayed you. You don't know yourselves how terribly you have been betrayed.' Shortly before, on 7 April 1919, he had written (on a postcard of himself) to a friend, 'I am now the commissar for propaganda, science, art, and a few other things. If I am allowed a few weeks' time I hope to accomplish something; but there is a bare possibility that it will only be a couple of days and then it will have been but a dream.' At the time of his murder on 2 May 1919 Landauer was fifty-six.

5.   Erwin Panofsky (1890–1969) is probably best known for his studies of Leonardo da Vinci, Dürer, and Galileo. He also wrote a stimulating essay on cinema: 'Style and Medium in the Motion Pictures' (originally in the *Bulletin of the Department of Arts and Archeology*, Princeton, 1934; reprinted – slightly revised – in *Critique*, Vol. 1, No. 3, January–February 1947; now available in Daniel Talbot, ed., *Film: An Anthology*, Berkeley and Los Angeles, 1966).

6.   Hermann Bossdorf, *Bahnmeister Tod* (written in Low German).

7.   Sirk's translations of the sonnets were published in Hamburg in 1922. The Brücke ('Bridge') group was founded in 1903, and brought together the early Expressionist painters – Heckel, Kirchner, Schmidt-Rottluff. Nolde and Pechstein affiliated to it for a time, as did Otto Müller, but these latter soon drifted away, and the group disbanded by 1913.

8.   Sirk translated *The Merry Wives of Windsor, The Tempest, Cymbeline*, and *Twelfth Night* (twice), as well as Pirandello's *Six Characters in Search of an Author*.

9.   *33 Jahre Bremer Schauspielhaus im Spiegel der Zeitkritik*, Bremen, n.d. (*c.* 1944), Carl Schünemann Verlag. This is a most useful source. It was, however, compiled during the Nazi period and is therefore often defective: for example, it may acknowledge that an unwelcome play such as the *Dreigroschenoper* was staged in the theatre in 1929, but says little or nothing about it, omitting, for instance, the fact that Sirk staged it.

10.   In an article written for a Leipzig newspaper at the time of his appointment to head the Altes Theater there, Sirk wrote about *Antony and Cleopatra*: 'I will never, above all, lose the exciting memory of the weeks in which I had to stage Shakespeare's *Antony and Cleopatra*, even if it only became a draft, a rough outline of what I felt. This world of political actors, inflated Caesars, soldiers, sailors and gypsies, and this extraordinary lady! And all under the drive of their hunger for power, their ambition (*Sinne*), their political fever, a world of terribly real flesh, which finally becomes spiritual through the death of the two most voluptuous people.

     'What a world! – I have never felt something similar in any other play, the geographical sphere right beside the spiritual. You get a sense of the globe, of the earth. You gaze from Europe to Asia, and further into the depths of Africa where, at the end of the earthly world, the Pyramids of the grave are waiting.' (Detlef Sierck, *Begegnung mit dem Genie, Leipziger Neueste Nachrichten*, 30 November 1929.) The Pyramids appear again in Sirk's films: in *Scandal in Paris* as a symbol of both power and death, and in *All that Heaven Allows*, referring to the treatment of widows in New England. Another translation of the whole article is printed in *Screen*, Vol. 12, No. 2.

11.   An allusion to a novel by Heinrich Mann, *Zwischen den Rassen* (*Between the Races*), 1907.

12.   Erwin Piscator (1893–1966) was one of the leading left-wing theatre directors in Weimar Germany. He used films in several of his stage productions. In 1934, in exile in the Soviet Union, he directed his only film, *The Revolt of the Fishermen*.

13.   Hanns Johst, who had been a pacifist at the end of the First World War, was the author of perhaps the most famous Nazi play, *Schlageter* (1932). Earlier

he had written the curious, quasi-Nazi *Thomas Paine* (1927). Subsequently he was for a time President of the Reichstheaterkammer, the Nazi Theatre Organization.

14. Alfred Hugenberg was head of the right-wing ex-servicemen's organization, the Steel Helmet, during the Weimar period. He became Vice-Chancellor in Hitler's cabinet in 1933. He was an important press baron, and owned Ufa (Universum Film Aktiengesellschaft).

15. Sirk remained with the Leipzig theatre until 1936.

16. Georg Kaiser (1878–1945) was the foremost playwright of German Expressionism. His most famous plays include *Gas* and *Oktobertag*. Kaiser, of course, had moved beyond Expressionism by this time. Two of Kurt Weill's songs from *The Silver Lake* are on a record KL 5056, sung by Lotte Lenya.

17. On 24 February 1933, the *Völkischer Beobachter*, which was the official Party daily, ran an anonymous article attacking the play. After various sallies against Kaiser, Weill, and Brecher and their 'salon Bolshevist friends', the commentator goes on: 'Detlef Sierck, who took on the production for the Leipzig Altes Theater ... and directed it, has rendered a service to the Berlin literary intelligentsia (*Literatentum*) and its outdated (*vorgestrigen*) intellectual satellites which stands to cost him very dear indeed.' (It is difficult to reproduce the violent and purely Nazi language of the original in English. J.H.)

18. In 1964, Hans Rothe wrote (to a German review which had done a feature on the *Silbersee*): 'Almost exactly 31 years ago I was a guest at the première in Leipzig of the *Silbersee*, when everyone who counted in the German theatre met together for the last time. And everyone knew this. The atmosphere there can hardly be described. It was "the last day of the greatest decade of German culture in the twentieth century". Brecher was the conductor. Sierck staged the production. The barracking and yelling were somewhat disturbing. But in spite of that it was a great evening, certainly the most impressive theatrical evening I have ever been present at.'

19. Otto Laubinger was the first President of the Reichstheaterkammer.

20. Merton Hodge, *The Wind and the Rain*; first published London, 1934; staged in October 1933. The Hodge play is set in a lodging house for male medical students in a Scottish university town.

2: German Films: 1935–1937

How did you manage finally to shift from the theatre to the cinema?

While I was still the managing director of the Altes Theater in Leipzig – it must have been 1934 – I got an offer to stage Shakespeare's *Twelfth Night* at the Berlin Volksbühne, which was one of the biggest theatres in Berlin. I wasn't really eager to do the play, because I'd staged it twice already. But I thought: this is a chance to do something in Berlin, at least. So I did a partly new translation of the play – although I did not communicate this to the people in charge of the writing department, because they were the most suspicious and Nazi of the lot. Then I staged the play in a musically realistic way. I even used the Brechtian three-quarter curtain. The sets were the main thing in the overall conception, and we built a cottage for Olivia which I think really smelt of England. The acting, too, was quite against my stage conscience: it was terribly realistic. And the new translation was also designed towards the same end, since it mainly consisted of prose. I tried to stage it in a movie way, crazily hoping against hope, ten times over, that some of the movie people, who were all in Berlin, would take note. Amazingly enough, two days later the Ufa producers showed up. The play was a big success. I had an interview at Ufa, and I was hired. At this time it was quite unusual for stage people to direct pictures at Ufa.

As I told you, in Leipzig I had been under constant attack ever since the Nazis came into power, and I had only survived because of Dr Goerdeler. But altogether it was impossible down there. I had no passport, and things were extremely bad. My idea was to get into pictures and emerge there as a completely new personage because – strange as it may seem – these movie people seemed to know nothing about my political past.

And then there was a strange system of what I call 'parallelisms'. You could have a very low political rating and a very high artistic rating at the same time, which is what I had. So perhaps even if one or two of the Ufa people did know about it, it didn't matter.

But Ufa was a very Nazi outfit, wasn't it? **1644399**

Strangely enough, no, it wasn't, not yet. It was still a privately owned company, and there weren't any Nazis in it at the time – there didn't have to be, because the Hugenberg people were very right-wing anyway. In 1934–35 the situation in the movies was still a lot better than in the theatre.

You are reported as having started out at Ufa making three short films: can you remember anything about these, because not even the titles are in the filmographies?

When I was taken on, the head of Ufa production, Mr Correll, gave me three playlets. I remember that one of these was called *Dreimal Liebe (Three Times Love)*, or something like that. At any rate, it told a story from three points of view: first from the point of view of the lover, then the husband, then the woman. I think this was the first time this method was used in the movies. It was taken up a number of times subsequently.

Was it your own script?

No, I was handed the script. But I changed the structure. And I changed the planned character of the sets a lot. You know, a set is an expression of the people in it, as well as the people being an expression of the set. As I'd had experience as a set designer, I felt quite strongly about this. Later on, in Hollywood, one of the big problems was the sets, because the work there was very much compartmentalized, which I wasn't used to. . . . At any rate, I managed to change the sets on this film, because now it is coming back to me, this was my third short piece for Ufa, and by now I realized they wanted me, and I knew I could do what I wanted.

Sequence of sketches by Sirk for one of his early shorts (1934–35); there is some similarity with a sequence in *Sleep, My Love* (1947)

In the Cahiers *interview*[1] *you say one of the others was Molière's* Le Malade Imaginaire.

Yes, I think it was, but I can't remember anything about the picture any more. I have some sketches I did for one of these short films, which I remember doing for my own continuity, but I can't recall which one they were for. I used sketches only right at the beginning. There are two types of directors. Reinhardt, for example, used sketches for directing on the stage, but I'm an improviser; I'm too much of an actor's director for this, and I soon abandoned them.

The only other thing I can remember about these shorts is that all three had Hans Schaufuss in them, and they must have been 30–40 minutes each.

Then you made your first feature, April, April! *in both German and Dutch. Did you shoot the Dutch version first, and was it in Holland?*

The Dutch version was first (*'T was één April*). I didn't go to Holland. I think my assistant shot about a couple of weeks of background shots in Holland, but both versions were made in Germany — with different casts.

Why two versions?

At the time, Ufa had a huge market abroad, and they often made films in two and even three versions: very often a Spanish version for Latin America, where their films sold a lot. I can't remember much about *April*, but there must have been some reason connected with it for doing the Dutch version. The drawback about shooting two versions — which I did again with *Hofkonzert* the next year (*La Chanson du Souvenir*) — was that one version inevitably suffered. You naturally couldn't give the same attention to both. And you couldn't change your angling, lighting, and so on, either. Maybe one guy was taller than his counterpart in the other version, so you just cut off half his head, or maybe the composition didn't look too good on one group.

So the first version, the Dutch one, is presumably the better one?

That's right. The German version was technically not so good. But *April* was only a B-picture, and it wasn't as serious as it was with the re-make of *Hofkonzert*.

Did you bring any actors with you from the stage?

Yes, several of the smaller parts were played by people I had been working with in the theatre, like Lina Carstens, Erhard Siedel, and Odette Orsy. Willi Winterstein, the cameraman, was a good technician, and it was all useful training for me. By the time I'd finished *April* I knew the technical stuff about picture-making. And by the time of *Hofkonzert* I knew about the camera and lighting. There is something the *Cahiers du Cinéma* say which pleased me very much, about how my camera became the people. I have a very mobile camera, whereas some directors, like Ford and Hawks, can work with an almost still camera.

After April *you did* Das Mädchen vom Moorhof *(The Girl from the Marsh Croft) from the Selma Lagerlöf novel. Why did you choose this? Were you interested in Lagerlöf?*

I didn't choose the story myself – but, as with the Ibsen which I did next (*Pillars of Society*), Lagerlöf was very well known. She had won the Nobel Prize. She was enormously popular in the belt running down from Scandinavia through Germany, but of course not at all in England. She is perhaps comparable to Knut Hamsun; she continues the tradition of the Icelandic sagas; she has monumental simplicity, which is good for pictures – and, as you know, a lot of pictures were made from her books. When I was in Hollywood I wrote a screenplay for Columbia based on another book by her, *The General's Ring*, but it wasn't filmed. The screenplay for *Das Mädchen vom Moorhof* deviated quite a bit from the original, and I thought it made a mistake in transferring Lagerlöf's story into a North German locale. People in Scandinavia are different from the Germans. The peasantry there are more highly educated than anywhere else in Europe.

Where was it shot?

Between Bremen and Hamburg, in a Protestant zone. The people there are stiff, silent people, so that aspect at least was all right.

One striking thing is that in spite of the rather gloomy story, the whole film takes place in bright sunshine, which is odd for you: I was expecting a storm or two.

I had to wait for the sun. The weather was very bad, as always in moor country. The film wasn't sensitive enough without full sunlight – or so the cameraman told me; perhaps I should have been more daring. It would have looked completely different in colour; just compare it with *Captain Lightfoot*.

Pillars of Society (Stützen der Gesellschaft) *seems to me to show a great advance compared with* Mädchen vom Moorhof. *Particularly, I thought you got some excellent transitions: the shots with the Norwegian flag, and the cut from the American West to Norway.*

I had learnt a lot in the meantime, and I had learned that what is important in picture-making is the ability to recognize a film in its continuity. During the shooting of *Schlussakkord* the following year I realized there has to be a sustained mood of acting, lighting, and so on, and you will see this style for the first time in *Schlussakkord*. But I had got a number of insights before that. This sustained mood is very important. Ford has this gift. And I think Hawks has it, too. It has nothing to do with the story. It is a matter of style. Angling is terribly important: I discovered this for the first time with *Pillars of Society*. The angles are the director's thoughts. The lighting is his philosophy. Even to this extent: long before Wittgenstein, I and some of my contemporaries learned to distrust language as a true medium and interpreter of reality. So I learned to trust my eyes rather more than the windiness of words.

I wanted to ask you about the Americanism in Germany after the First World War, which one sees very much in Brecht. In Pillars of Society *I was struck by the way you'd expanded the whole American element and made it much more prominent: was this still a major cultural phenomenon in the mid-thirties? And where did you shoot it?*

We shot it in Germany, although we went to an island in the Baltic called Bornholm for a couple of weeks, and that's where we shot that huge storm. But I was always very interested in America, and I was enthusiastic about things American: that's why I put in that American episode there. And I think that's why I got in Klaren to do the writing, because he knew about America, I think he'd lived there for a while.

You know, I liked being able to shoot outside on this picture. I could never have got the time or money to do something like the storm sequence in Hollywood. We got soaked and drenched, nearly drowned doing that storm – but it came off. You can't fake a storm like that. I think if I'd been an American I'd have become a director of Westerns, because this is the American cinema *par excellence*, and you can get outside all the time, which is where I like being.

Quite apart from the American aspect of the film, I was surprised how iconoclastic it is: for example, you expose the figure of Consul Bernick right from the moment he is introduced at the unveiling of the statue; you have divided up the onlookers into two groups – the applauding bourgeoisie and the hostile sailors and proletariat. How did you get away with things like that under the Nazis? And why did you shift the thing away from Ibsen's method of introducing the various elements?

The treatment of Bernick is all part of my attitude towards suspense. I don't like to leave the audience in the dark. Besides, the Ibsen play is old-fashioned in structure. It needed adapting. And I was trying to get away from the theatre, and from literature. The critics all thought this was sacrilege at the time, because they were literary-minded; but, to their surprise, the picture was a big success. No one complained about it politically. You could still get away with extraordinary things under the Nazis. It took time for everything to seize up, and at Ufa there was still a certain amount of room for manoeuvre.

No one complained about those crowd scenes, and the way you shot the flags?

No, no one minded. This was perhaps out of reverence for Ibsen; even though they attacked me for changing him a bit, they were still

The world of small-town pretence and deceit: Heinrich George (Bernick) with Suse Graf (left) as Dina Dorf and Maria Krahn as Bernick's wife in *Stützen der Gesellschaft*

stuck with their reverence for him. But I'm glad you got the iconoclasm in it, because in a way it ties up with some of my earlier work, and particularly my staging of *The Silver Lake*, which *was* absolute suicide. You know, when I had finished this picture I thought it was going to get me into trouble. Every picture had to be screened by a group of Nazi bureaucrats, who were an awful bunch of people who just wanted to get near the movie stars. Anyway, one day Mr Correll called me up to his office just after the picture was completed. I was trembling: the whole business is going to start all over again, just like in Leipzig, I thought. But no ... the Führer himself had seen the picture, Mr Correll told me, and had liked it a lot – you know Mr Hitler was very keen on the pictures: he was running a movie nearly every night. I had a feeling of both relief and deep depression: it must be a bad picture if this man likes it. ... I was worried, so I asked a couple of friends who had seen it, and they said it was all right.

I haven't seen Schlussakkord, *your next movie. I read something*

*about it saying 'It goes all the way from astrology to Beethoven's
Ninth', which is quite a long way – what kind of film was it?*

Well, it has sensational music – big pieces of the Ninth
Symphony.... The clairvoyant was a kind of take-off of a famous
clairvoyant who, people said, was advising Hitler, and even running
Germany. Can you imagine it? It was ridiculous.

But *Schlussakkord* is rather an important film in my career. When
I got the script, I got a smell of a tremendous success. The treatment
had been done by a man called Oberländer, who was a well-known
screen-writer. But when he saw my finished version of the script – I
went right through it, re-writing it – he took his name off it. The
studio weren't happy, because he was well known. But he absolutely
insisted. He could not see the novelty of my finished script, the music
or anything. I knew I had a success. Now, it is obvious that a script
by myself, or by Oberländer, can't be compared, *as writing*, to a
novel by Selma Lagerlöf or a play by Ibsen.

This was the first time in the cinema I went off the literary thing. You
will have seen that my stage record is very literary. *Schlussakkord*
was a tremendous deviation from my stage work. But it illustrates
very well the need for cinema values, distinct from literary (or stage)
values. After the Lagerlöf and Ibsen pictures I needed something
more *kino* – I needed to go back to my early impressions of the
cinema, to melodrama. When I was a young child I used to go to the
cinema a lot, particularly to a small cinema called the Théâtre Royal
in Hamburg, where they ran a lot of melodramas, mainly Danish
ones. And now I felt I had to go back to those early days and
recapture something of the atmosphere of those films, and of the
happiness they gave me as a child. I realized I had to make a complete break with my theatrical past. I had realized that the cinema
and the theatre are two completely different media before I went
into pictures at all. But at the beginning I was terribly tied to literature. From *Schlussakkord* onwards I got right away and tried to
develop a cinema style. I began to understand that the camera is the
main thing here, because there is *emotion* in the motion pictures.
Motion is emotion, in a way it can never be in the theatre.

You know, this film made more money than any other Ufa production for years. Up until then I had been watched as an over-
intellectual young man. They weren't quite sure after the Lagerlöf

Adults and children, toys and the theatre: Peter Bosse (right) entertains his foster-father, Willy Birgel, and his real mother, Maria von Tasnady, who has been hired as his governess (*Schlussakkord*)

and Ibsen pictures. But *Pillars of Society* became a success, which they didn't expect. And then right after *Schlussakkord* they knew I had the golden touch, which you have to have in movies.

You put in another American opening here, too?

Yes, I wrote that into the script myself, the New York bit. I had a shot there very like one I got in *A Time to Love and a Time to Die*. You remember the shot of the man's face frozen in the snow which is just thawing, and he seems to be crying? Well, in the opening of *Schlussakkord* there is a shot of a mask lying in the snow – it is New Year's Day – and at first it seems to be the face of a man.

It looks as though you had fantastic studio facilities on the film.

I did: all those huge sets – Central Park, the churches – are all studio sets.

Schlussakkord *is a big musical film, like* Hofkonzert, *which you did next?*

Yes, much more so. *Hofkonzert* was a genre movie; *Schlussakkord* was a melodrama, my first, but a certain kind of melodrama, while *Hofkonzert* was traditional. Melodrama means music plus drama – we must come back to this later. . . .

Schlussakkord was a powerful title in German.[2] All the translations lose the ambiguity of the German. And although *Dreiklang* (*Triad*) – a project I had slightly later – had nothing to do with music, Ufa liked the title, and took it on partly because of the musical thing of *Schlussakkord*.

Can you tell me about Hofkonzert (Court Concert)?

It was a piece of Viennese pastry. After the heaviness of *Schlussakkord*, I felt the need to do something light, and that's why I tried it – it needed a light touch. I shot it in Würzburg in the summer of 1936. You can see from the stills what a big budget movie it was. I had Martha Eggerth in it, who was a famous soprano at the time – and she did both the German and French versions. I was able to do some experimenting with light and the camera in it. I had a very good cameraman: Weihmayr did a great job on this picture, and I kept him for the rest of my German pictures. Edmund Nick, who did the music, was a great person to work with, and he was an excellent composer.[3]

But here having to do two versions was extremely serious, because – unlike *April* – this was a big picture, and a very subtle one. And there is a great difference in the languages: French is much further removed from German than Dutch is – and this was terribly important. I had to do a completely different cutting on the French version, largely because of the language difference. I even remember asking Correll not to release the French version.

Zu Neuen Ufern[4] *reminded me a bit of* Captain Lightfoot: *at least in its attitude to the English; I was quite struck by the attack on the British ruling class in* Zu Neuen Ufern, *and by the rather subtle distinctions you got in between old and new merchants and declining aristocracy – it's quite tough in this way.*

'A piece of Viennese pastry': statues, shadows and pompousness in *Das Hofkonzert*

Yes, it is. It was meant to be. It is a piece of social criticism, of the kind I like. Some people perhaps thought it was anti-English, but there is much more to it than that. There is the same sort of social criticism in this picture as in *La Habanera*. Now, I hate the term 'social criticism' because it has become a cliché, but there doesn't seem to be any other expression to describe this kind of picture. Besides, the word 'criticism' has two sides to it in English. What I am doing in a picture like this is just showing things; the criticism has to start in the audience. I am merely trying to awaken the audience to a consciousness of conditions. It is more a piece of social *awareness*: it remains in the realms of signs and symbols; it is pointing to things. It just presents things.

In fact *Zu Neuen Ufern* is a good picture to talk about because it has two elements which are fundamental to my picture-making: this aspect of social awareness, and also the kind of character I am interested in, the part played by Willy Birgel (Sir Albert Finsbury). The type of character I always have been interested in, in the theatre as well as in the movies, and which I also tried to retain in melo-

Making a star: Zarah Leander trying to survive in a nineteenth-century Sydney music-hall (*Zu Neuen Ufern*)

drama, is the doubtful, the ambiguous, the uncertain. Uncertainty, and the vagueness of men's aims, are central to many of my films, however hidden these characteristics may be. I am interested in circularity, in the circle – people arriving back at the place they started out from. This is why you will find what I call tragic rondos in many of my films, people going in circles. This is what most of my characters are doing. Hence my attraction to Macbeth, who is one of these characters; so, for example, are Herod in Hebbel's *Herodes und Mariamne*, Maximilian in Werfel's *Juarez und Maximilian*, and many of Pirandello's characters. In my pictures, I think this first appears in *Zu Neuen Ufern*. The Willy Birgel character is one of these: vague, uncertain, ambiguous, going round – around himself . . . and hopeless.

Only recently I read a play by Edward Bond, *Early Morning*, and I found in it a more powerful image for what I want to say than I have been able to find myself:

Arthur: 'D'you dream? – So do I. D'you dream about the mill? There are men and women and children and cattle and birds and horses pushing a mill. They're grinding other cattle and people and children: they push each other in. Some fall in. It grinds their bones, you see. The ones pushing the wheel, even the animals, look up at the horizon. They stumble. Their feet get caught up in the rags and dressings that slip down from their wounds. They go round and round. At the end they go very fast. They shout. Half of them run in their sleep. Some are trampled on. They're sure they're reaching the horizon. . . .'[5]

I liked the whole sequence of shots connected with the big mirror which Viktor Staal buys for Zarah Leander when they get married.

I can't quite remember the mirror business in *Zu Neuen Ufern*. But the mirror is the imitation of life. What is interesting about a mirror is that it does not show you yourself as you are, it shows you your own opposite. Do you know Strindberg's *Dream Play*? You know the story of this play: a man arriving with some flowers and calling to a woman whom he cannot see. You hear the echo of his call, and then the echo of the echo. And then the man disappears, and that is the end. This is like the mirror of the mirror, the imitation of the imitation of life. It is a surrealist play, and Strindberg is the source of many later things in the theatre – and in picture-making.

The first of Sirk's 'doubtful, ambiguous and uncertain' characters in the cinema: Willy Birgel (Sir Albert Finsbury) contemplates himself in the rain-spattered window shortly before his suicide in *Zu Neuen Ufern*

Somebody like Godard, I think, has drawn to a great extent on Strindberg.

But there is one other – technical – thing I should say about *Zu Neuen Ufern*, and this is that I had built up certain defences of my own by this time. You always have to guard against the cutters, and I had started cutting in the camera by this time, so as not to give the cutters too much stuff. This is a dangerous thing, and with *Zu Neuen Ufern* I was given the chance to re-shoot scenes where it was necessary. In Hollywood it was rather the other way round: they always gave me plenty of film, but they were much more reluctant about shooting re-takes. But by this time I had developed the habit so well I felt safe in employing it. And, as you know, the picture turned out to be a big success, and Zarah Leander had a huge hit in it; overnight it made her into the biggest star in Germany.

So you went straight on to make La Habanera *with her after that?*

That's right. Now, this was another bit of what I have called social criticism. The Ferdinand Marian character (Don Pedro) whom Zarah Leander marries owns everything on the island, and is trying to conceal a plague which is ravaging it, because he is in league with the big American fruit companies and he thinks that if people abroad find out about the plague they will stop buying his fruit. It was an anti-capitalist movie, which went down well in Germany at the time.

Gerhard Menzel, who did the script with you, was a rather well-known writer, wasn't he?

He was a very gifted writer, and a very highly paid one. He had won the Kleistpreis, which was the biggest literary prize in Germany. But then he wasted his talents. He had been one of the big hopes of German literature for a time. Later on he became a big Nazi.

Was he a Nazi when he worked with you?

Well, I couldn't say. I remember asking him about it, and he kept on saying, 'I'm not a Nazi, I'm not a Nazi', but by then it was awfully hard to know what some people were.

I was a little apprehensive when I noticed you opening the movie with a bullfight.

Well, this is irony dressed up as romanticism. I don't think it's out of place there. You must remember that this was 1937. This was the first bullfight in a German picture; it was not the cliché element it later perhaps became. And I think it set off the contrast between the allure of the Ferdinand Marian character and his achievement. Menzel wanted to have the bullfight in a big arena. I didn't. I moved it into a small village, with a tiny arena, to make it more raw, and this way it showed up better the shallowness of Don Pedro's heroic pose. The bullfight sets the scene for the gloom that is to come. And it resumes much of the falseness of the situation. You see, irony is an element in a number of my pictures ... this is something we can come back to later. I got some irony into *Pillars of Society*. The very title there is ironic – it was ironic in Ibsen's intentions, of course, and I've made it maybe even more ironic in the picture. The George character (Bernick), with his own capitalistic thinking, is instru-

Light, heat, orchids and gloom: the breakdown of the marriage between Ferdinand Marian (Don Pedro de Avila) and Zarah Leander in *La Habanera*

mental in almost destroying his own world, and killing his son. And the same in *La Habanera*: Ferdinand Marian brings about his own ruin, and death in this case – which I make very explicit.

When he collapses by the pool at the party someone actually says, 'Don Pedro has buried himself.'

That's right. Like Consul Bernick, his capitalistic machinations and his deceit, his trying to hide things, bring his world down.

It is rather striking how the last sequence of the film, your last German film, is like the last sequence of Imitation of Life, *your last American film. The scene on the boat in* La Habanera *is very like the one in the car at the funeral in* Imitation of Life.

Well, Zarah Leander's feelings on that boat are not entirely linear. She has been in the place ten years, the ten best years of her life. As

51

she looks back she is aware that she is getting out of rotten – *but definitely interesting* – circumstances. Her feelings are most ambiguous. I think in the end of *Imitation of Life* the ambiguity is more external: the irony is in the eye of the audience.

Can I clear up the various other films you are credited as having had something to do with? What's the position about Liebling der Matrosen?

I did write this, for a Viennese company, in order to get some money abroad. I did not shoot it, but I introduced a new director from the stage, Hans Hinrich, who directed it, and then did *Dreiklang.*

Dreiklang *is credited as your* idea. *What in fact did you do?*

It was a film I was very keen on making. I had written a script myself, based on two Russian stories: *The Shot* by Pushkin, and *First Love* by Turgenev. I had first done a treatment of *The Shot*, and then I decided to use the Turgenev story as the basis, integrating the duel from the Pushkin, which I needed for my story.

I think the treatment was good. It was a very interesting story, typical of a certain trend in my work. It is a love story, but one of those off-love stories I have often tried to make – and this was the first one. It is also a story of love in extreme circumstances, love socially conditioned. Not just a love story, but one where the social circumstances condition the love. The structure of society in which this happening of love is embedded is just as important as the love itself.

In the Turgenev story a father and his son are both in love with the same woman. My treatment concentrated on the older man, who is more interesting, being much more uncertain than his son in his love, as is always the case in life. I have often tried to work round the themes of love, and the social conditioning on love, which I had in *Dreiklang.*

I picked the locations and everything for the picture, the dresses, the sets, everything – and then I left. *Dreiklang* was a good title, particularly in German. You know what it means? Three notes played together, a triad.

'Getting out of rotten – but definitely interesting – circumstances': Zarah Leander with Karl Martell at the end of *La Habanera*. The last shot of Sirk's last German film

What about Wiltons Zoo, *which is mentioned in the* Cahiers *interview?*

I certainly was given a script on this, and as I recall it, a very good script. I think I planned to make it after *Dreiklang.* When *La Habanera* was finished, and the preparations had been made for *Dreiklang,* I left Germany, ostensibly to research locations for *Wiltons Zoo.*

Can you tell me how you left, because it isn't at all clear from the sources?

Well, as I told you, I had long since decided to get out because life was becoming absolutely impossible. But, of course, I had no passport. After *Zu Neuen Ufern,* I suggested *La Habanera,* to be shot on location in Tenerife – and by now I was an influential director, with a big star, Zarah Leander, and so my suggestion was adopted at

Sirk (in cap) directing Leander and Martell in the final sequence of *La Habanera*

once. As far as I remember, I got a travel document to leave Germany to make the picture, but I didn't get a passport, which you needed to be able to get a permit to enter the States. So I went back and did the editing of *La Habanera* in Germany, and then sought, and got permission to go abroad again to look for locations on *Wiltons Zoo* – and for this I was given a passport.

So I went to Rome, where Mrs Sirk was, and pretended to fall ill. The Ufa people kept ringing from Berlin every day, and Mrs Sirk kept telling them I was too ill to answer the phone. Because I was trying to figure out what to do. I'd decided to leave Germany for good, but the passport I'd got had a time limit on it, and it was all a question of getting some American documents in time. Anyway, one day Ufa called again to say that the producer of *Dreiklang* was coming to Rome the following day to see me.

The thing was that Italy was a Fascist country, and I thought 'They've got a deal on with Hitler, and it could be dangerous.' We had to do something. So Mrs Sirk got on to the hotel owner who maybe even was a Fascist, but he had one thing going for him which was that he absolutely hated the Germans. And once he realized what we were after, he said his wife's sister's cousin was a nun and maybe she could do something. So these nuns said they would put me up in the hospital to make it look good. As you know, I had been brought up a Protestant, and I wasn't used to this, but the nun told me it was all right, it was only going to be a white lie to save me from the

Germans. Anyway, I was lying there in bed, looking rather healthy, because I'd never been ill in my life, and feeling rather worried about this fact. So one of the nuns said, 'Now, we'll fix something up for you. You put this hot water bottle under your blanket; we'll bring it along just before this guy turns up, you put your hands on it, and when the man comes in whip your hand out and shake his hand, and it'll be very, very hot.' And so I said, 'Sister, you're just great, couldn't I hire you as a gag-man for my movies?' But I don't think she even knew what I was talking about. Anyway, the next day the producer turned up, and I stick out my hand, and he says, 'My God, you're ill, you're *really* ill. You must take care, and we need you, you're a great director, and so on.' So I said to him, 'Why don't you try and get somebody else to do the picture?' (*Dreiklang*), and he said, 'No, no, I wouldn't think of it. We need you.' I tell you, he was deeply impressed, because he was a Protestant like me, and with all these nuns standing around looking solemn telling him I was really ill, he was absolutely convinced. It was lucky, because he had come down in a special plane from Berlin with two guys from the police who were waiting at the door to carry me out and put me in the plane back to Germany if I was fit to be moved.

Anyway, he went back to Berlin, and I got up and wrote a letter to Dr Correll telling him what I thought of the Nazis and everything, and saying I would not go back. Then I booked Mrs Sirk and myself on a plane to Zurich, and mailed the letter just as I was leaving.

NOTES

1. *Cahiers du Cinéma* 189 (April 1967): so far as I know, the only extensive interview with Sirk on the cinema in any language (the interview dates from 1964).
2. *Schlussakkord* means both 'final chord' and 'concluding agreement' (or 'arrangement'); cf. p. 56 (*Accord Final*).
3. Edmund Nick's most famous work is probably the satirical cantata *Leben in dieser Zeit* (1931), which he wrote with Erich Kästner, the author of *Emil and the Detectives*.
4. *Nu Zeuen Ufern:* lit. *To New Shores.* The film appears to have been released in the English-speaking world as *Life Begins Anew.* To avoid confusion, I have kept references to it in German.
5. Edward Bond, *Early Morning*, Calder & Boyars, London, 1968, p. 68 (scene II).

3: France and Holland: 1938–1939

What did you do then? The information on this period is highly contradictory.

I was headed for Paris, but en route we stopped off in Zurich. And there a friend invited me to a party. I don't much like parties, but I needed to make all the contacts I could, so I went along. There were several movie people there, including the man who had distributed *Schlussakkord* in Switzerland, Mr Weissmann. He had a brother-in-law called Rosenkranz who wanted to make a picture, and Weissmann asked me if I would work on it, and supervise it, since Rosenkranz had never made a film. Weissmann loved the title *Schlussakkord* and asked me if he could lift the title in French and call Rosenkranz's picture *Accord Final* (which isn't such a good title in French). So I said, OK, why not, since it belonged to Ufa, and I didn't care. So I went to Paris, at least with the prospect of some work, which I badly needed, because I'd left Germany with almost no money. And I 'supervised' the picture.

Can you remember much about it?

No, I can't. There was an excellent cameraman, I recall. Jacques Natanson wrote the dialogue. And there was some music – it was about the Paris Conservatoire.

There was another script I worked on at the time, called *L'on revient toujours* . . . but I don't know what happened to it.

Anyway, I'd made a break with Germany and the Germans. Ufa

brought a suit against me in France for breaking my contract, and they took my name off the films I had made in Germany – so they sometimes appeared without any director's credit at all. I think this lawsuit was an added reason for my working under pseudonyms and anonymity, like on *Accord Final*, and then going off to Holland.

I remember in Paris we were more or less in hiding. We were staying in a small hotel, going very carefully, because we had enough to live on for two or three months at most. I thought we had got away from the Germans. Then one day the phone rang, and it was my old producer from Ufa, Duday. He invited me out to lunch, and I accepted, as I hadn't had a good meal for a long time. He tried to persuade me to go back to Germany: 'Your career is in Germany. You belong in Germany, and the Nazis are here to stay: they will soon control the whole of Europe,' he told me. So I said I did not want to go back, and I told him about the letter I'd written to Mr Correll. 'Don't worry,' he said, 'no-one knows about that – Correll didn't show it to anyone. In fact, I've got a personal letter for you from Dr Goebbels.'

What was in it?

It said I should come back to Germany, and I would be forgiven. It said I had a great future as a director in Germany, but it was rather threatening, too; it said nothing would happen to me if I went back to the Reich, but at the same time it was written in an almost military style.

Have you still got it?

Have I hell. I flushed it straight down the first lavatory.

After that they left you alone?

Yes, they did, except for the lawsuit.

I did one other thing in France. I was approached to finish a film of Renoir's, a kind of two-reeler, *Une Partie de Campagne* – a magnificent torso, and a great temptation, but I felt at the same time it would be impossible.

Why?

Well, Renoir is a great director, and it would be extremely tough to match styles with him. His lighting, for a start, is very different from my own style of lighting. And, while you can work on things you are cold about, it is another matter to operate on something you love – this I couldn't do. Of course, it was a temptation, but a temptation of quite a\ different kind from, say *M*, or *Caligari*, or other things which were offered to me to re-make at other times.

Can you tell me more about this: what were you asked to do – and what did you envisage doing?

I was asked to make it into a feature-length picture. I had the craziest ideas for fixing it up. I tried to write a second part to it. I also thought of framing what Renoir had shot as a picture within a picture, and I don't know what. Although I thought it was perfect the way it was, I was still seduced.

Did you discuss it with Renoir at all?

No, I didn't. I never knew him. But his directing had a great influence on me – and this goes right back to my theatre days. I think his films influenced even my stage work – this Mozartian touch he has. And then he also has an eye like a painter. . . . When I saw *Nana* I thought it was the greatest thing in the world. I also like his American movies very much indeed. *The Southerner* I really loved.

Then you went to Holland and shot Boefje*?*

That's right. You remember I had made *April* in Dutch, and I believe it had done all right. I got an offer to do *Boefje*, which was based on a famous Dutch novel with that title. I wrote the script with Carl Zuckmayer, a then rather well-known German playwright, who was an émigré, like myself – and he has a story about meeting me in Paris in his book, which is somewhere there on my shelves, of which I have no recollection. . . .[1]

I shot the whole picture myself in Holland, but it was edited after I left and I've never seen the final version. It was released after my

Boefje: Annie van Ees (left) as Boefje, Guus Brox as Pietje Puck, Albert van Dalsum as the priest

departure, because Mrs Sirk and I left Holland on the last day of shooting, on the last boat to get out of Holland, the *Staatendam.* . . . As far as I can remember, the only interesting thing about it is that the lead part of the boy is played by a girl, Annie van Ees, who had done the part on the stage. But it was a ridiculously small-budget film.

NOTE

1. Carl Zuckmayer, *Als Wär's ein Stück von Mir*, Vienna, 1966, p. 119, writes that he and Sirk were walking in front of Nôtre Dame in Paris when they heard the bells ringing to announce the election of Cardinal Pacelli as Pope Pius XII, whereupon (according to Zuckmayer) they both knelt down in the square to give thanks. 'Pacelli was an awful man. I can't believe the story' (Sirk). The English edition of Zuckmayer's memoirs, *A Part of Myself* (Secker and Warburg, 1970) omits the story entirely, without indicating the cut.

4: America I: 1939–1948

You went to America originally on a contract with Warners?

Yes. Warners hired me to re-make *Zu Neuen Ufern*. The telegram arrived while I was shooting *Boefje*.

What happened? The sources seem to indicate that you shot a re-make, which was then suppressed.

No, I didn't. The original idea was to buy the Ufa version and re-make it. I did re-write the story. I changed the Birgel part into an older man, I made him the father of the girl, and created a kind of interesting non-sexual love affair between the girl and the father. I think it was a rather modern relationship: the girl's love was not dependent on sex. It was a many-layered relationship. By changing it like this, I felt I strengthened the dependency of the girl on her father, and thus the reasons why she was prepared to go to prison in Australia instead of him. I think the re-write was probably even better than the original. I liked the father–daughter angle ... and I made the man much more ambiguous than in the Ufa film. He was still very attractive to women, though older: he was an ageing Don Juan. At the same time, he was capricious with old age, which was an interesting angle. Letting her go to prison instead of him was a terrible thing, but he is too weak to speak up. He knows if he goes to prison he will be finished when he comes out ... women will no longer be fascinated by him. He is a man who cannot get out of his circle, always coming back to his beloved self, trying to break out, but unable to do so.

And so, since he was older, conversely, the girl became younger – and I think this improved it, too. Because I was happier with a younger girl. In a way Zarah Leander was perhaps a little bit old for the part, but she was a special case.

Then things began to close in – this was before Pearl Harbor. Apparently Warners didn't want to do a re-make of a German picture, so it never got made, and I had one of the very short contracts, which I think was terminated after one year. There were a lot of lay-offs. Business was bad.

So, with my last 1,000 dollars I went and bought a small chicken farm in the San Fernando Valley. I spent a year or more on this farm and in some ways, although I was completely broke, it was maybe my happiest time in America. Then I sold it and bought an alfalfa farm in Pomona County, where we also grew avocados, and had a few cows. I spent about two years on this farm, and I liked the people out there a lot. And I was in the countryside, where I like being, among horses, cows, chickens. I thought my American movie career was probably over, and eventually the Hitler business would be finished and I could go back to pictures in Germany.

There is a report that you were about to go to the San Francisco Opera about this time – is that right?

Yes. Just before Pearl Harbor, the head of the San Francisco Opera, Mr Mirola, approached me for a project. Apart from his annual festival, he was also forming a repertory company for light opera, which was to include things like Mozart's *Singspiele*. He wanted me to head the company, and the programme was going to include *Zar und Zimmermann* (*Tsar and Carpenter*) by Lortzing, some operettas by Offenbach, *Die Fledermaus* by Strauss, and a couple of early Mozart pieces. I was quite enthusiastic. I thought: well, OK, I'll go back to the theatre. It was a good salary and I liked San Francisco. Everything was ready. Mirola had got all the backers together. We met in Lucy's Restaurant, right opposite the Paramount Studios. And we were there in the middle of lunch, with the contract all ready, when we heard a roar from the Paramount lot, and a crowd of extras came out of the gates shouting 'Pearl Harbor!' And Mirola said, 'We'd better wait.' I very vividly remember being knocked down by fate. . . .

How did the job come up in the first place?

Mirola had heard about me from Eggerth's husband, Kiepura. You remember Martha Eggerth had been the star in *Hofkonzert*, and she and her husband carried weight in the opera and singing world.

Did the opera people ever come back to you afterwards?

No. It was a period of sheer hysteria after Pearl Harbor, and nobody was willing to put up money for something like an opera. So I went back to the alfalfa farm again.

How did you come to sign up with Columbia – and when was it?

I had to sell the second farm, because after Pearl Harbor I couldn't hire any labour to harvest the alfalfa, and I knew I couldn't go on being a farmer. I naturally got very little money for the farm, because it was a bad moment.

About this time the movie industry decided to hire all the emigrants from France. Paul Kohner, my agent, persuaded me to sign a contract with Columbia – this must have been about mid-1942, and I think Heinz Harold, who had been one of Reinhardt's collaborators, also had some influence in the thing. I was hired separately – and as a writer, not a director. I got about 150 dollars a week, which was nothing in Hollywood. And this was a seven-year contract. I don't know if you know about these seven-year contracts, but they are the most impossible things in the whole world.

Were you very much involved in the German émigré world in Hollywood? Because this transfer of such an amazing group of people – Reinhardt, Jessner, Thomas Mann, Lang, Lorre, Werfel, Brecht – has always struck me as one of the most extraordinary cultural events of the century.

Well, I tell you the main thing was that nearly all of them were living in the past, because they had very little to do, or were often completely out of work altogether. But a few of them managed to make the transition rather well: I think the most brilliant of all at making the move from Europe was Renoir. Lang also managed it well.

Can I ask you a bit about your relationship with America before you got there? Apart from all the American elements in your German pictures, there seems to be a good bit of Henry James in Interlude, *thematically; and, indeed, there seems to be a constant element in your work of the relations between America and Europe.*

Yes, we should talk about that a little. There were, I think, three or four things in American literature – now this is quite apart from the American movies – which influenced me. The first was Melville. Melville was a revelation to me. I would almost like to put him next to Kafka. And for a long time I planned to make a movie out of one of the Piazza Tales, but I never did. Then the second one was Henry James whom I read, I think, slightly under the influence of Flaubert. *The Turn of the Screw* made a big impression on me, and I still consider it one of the most important books by an American author, and in its ambiguity really ahead of its time. I wish I could have made it into a movie.[1] The third was Faulkner: he was a very early influence on my outlook – even before I read *Pylon*. And then there were other people like Sherwood Anderson. Now I remember that sequence in *Zu Neuen Ufern* you mentioned about the mirror (see p. 48) – this was taken from a sequence in a book by Sherwood Anderson which I had just read at the time, but I'd completely forgotten about it. I was very much under the influence of Anglo-Saxon literature at that time. I remember that my friend Karl Lerbs, who translated *Pylon* into German and put me on to the story, earlier gave me a translation of a Sherwood Anderson story he was working on called *The Egg*. And then a favourite project of mine for a movie was Sherwood Anderson's *Dark Laughter*, and I also wanted to do Nabokov's *Laughter in the Dark*.[2] It is a very melodramatic tale. I wrote a treatment of it, and took it to the Hays Office, but they turned it down. The Sherwood Anderson I also planned to do in America, but it never came off.

All these things formed my vision of America. You know, I was in love with America, and I often have a great nostalgia for it. Not for Hollywood, but for the West, for Oregon and the North-West in

Church and State in *Hitler's Madman*: Al Shean (priest) and John Carradine
(Heydrich)

particular. I think I was one of the few German émigrés who came to
America with a certain background of reading about the country,
and a great interest in it – and I was about the only one who got
around and about. I used to travel whenever I could, whereas most of
the others sat around in Hollywood talking about the good old days
and never saw the country. That's why I was so happy living on a
farm, because I liked the country, and the people out there.

When I was at Universal I had a plan to make a sequence of films
about America, mainly about middle-class America and aspects of
the society I was interested in. But it did not come off as I had hoped.

How did you get assigned to Hitler's Madman *– not a Columbia
picture at all?*

I was approached with the project by an old friend, Rudi Joseph.
Rudi's brother, Al Joseph, had been working with Emil Ludwig,[3]
who was a well-known German émigré, and they had a treatment on
Heydrich, who had just been killed. The picture was set up entirely
by a group of German émigrés: Brettauer, a man who had financed
many important pictures in Germany (including *M*), provided the
backing; and Seymour Nebenzal produced it, with Rudi Joseph.

I was offered the picture, which was to be shot at some speed: I
was given one week's shooting time. It was specifically presented to
me as a very low-budget film, not even a B-feature, but a C- or D-
feature. I realized that it was both a chance and a danger. It could be

useful, and it might launch me. Or it could stick me as a B-feature director. And when this happens to you, no matter how good you are, you can just get stuck. Ulmer, for example, I think is a very good director, but he got stuck with B-features all his time in Hollywood.

Now, *Cahiers* have a note there saying something about how John Carradine must have been strange as Heydrich. Well, I can tell you he wasn't strange at all, because I had met Heydrich, and he and Carradine were very alike. In fact John Carradine *was* Heydrich.

How on earth did you meet Heydrich?

I met him at a party – but I'll come back to that in a minute. . . . Carradine was a stage actor and, more particularly, a Shakespearian stage actor, with a reputation of going overboard. A lot of Nazis behaved like Shakespearian actors. I did not know Heydrich well, but I had met him at a party in Berlin. It must have been one of the awful parties Ufa were always throwing. . . . Anyway, I didn't know who the heck he was, but being a very optical man, I got a good impression of his face, and it was very interesting. The thing was that Heydrich had been in the German Navy – and now I have to tell you something else about myself, which is that I started out at the German Naval Academy at Murwik, in North Germany. I went there when I was drafted towards the end of the First World War. I hated the idea of being a foot-soldier, and I think my father knew some people and he pulled a few strings to get me into Murwik. You can imagine what it was like in 1917–18. . . . Anyway, it was better than being a foot-soldier. Heydrich had been there, too – but I think he was younger than I was. The point was that anyone who'd been there was considered a colleague of anyone else who'd been there. He must have heard I'd been to Murwik, and so he came over to me at this party. He was in mufti, but he had the Nazi button and, as I said, he looked and behaved just like Carradine. He had the same edginess of speech. Now, Carradine was not a very good movie actor, but he was excellent for the part. He had a certain dry theatricality, which is just what I wanted. And Pat Morison is very good, too. . . . Have you seen the picture?

No, unfortunately, I haven't. What is the confusion about the title: Hitler's Madman/Hitler's Hangman*?*

Lighting: John Carradine, dying as *Hitler's Madman*

I think the original idea was to call it *Hitler's Hangman*, but this title had to be scrapped because of the Lang picture (*Hangmen Also Die*). My picture was started before the Lang went into production. I shot the film in a week, on schedule – this must have been late summer 1942: we would never have taken on the picture if we'd known about the Lang project. Now, I had shot the film almost like a documentary, since this seemed the style best suited to the theme, and given the very limited shooting time. Louis B. Mayer saw the picture and liked it very much, and he bought it. This was the first outside picture that MGM ever bought. And on the strength of it Metro hired Seymour Nebenzal, the producer, and they wanted to hire me as well, but Harry Cohn refused to allow it. However, when Mayer bought the film for distribution, he asked me if I would shoot some re-takes he wanted done, and for this I was given plenty of time, and the MGM facilities. But my feeling is that these re-takes detracted from the documentary character of the movie. It was an unsuccessful attempt to convert it into another kind of picture. For various reasons, the picture got stuck in Metro's ... it was lying around for a very long time, and it wasn't released until 1943, after the Lang had come out, and it was then re-titled *Hitler's Madman*. I remember while I was shooting the re-takes on the Metro lot a man came up to me and asked me if I was Douglas Sirk, the guy who made *Hitler's Hangman*. I said I was, and he said, 'My name is King Vidor, and I liked your picture very much. You know about composition and lighting, and I hope you won't let yourself get demoralized, because I think you could have a future in store if you just persevere.' I tell you, this was encouragement – and I needed it, mainly because of my situation at Columbia.

You know, the most demoralizing thing was being prevented from working. I went to Harry Cohn and asked him to let me make a picture, but he refused. He told me to my face that because I was under contract, he was the man who would decide what – and if – I would do.

I've just looked at the filmography here, and I must add in one thing, which is the name of Eugen Shuftan. I brought him in on the picture, but he wasn't allowed to work in America because of the guild, so we had to bring in Greenhalgh who, I see here, had the credit. On *Hitler's Madman* it didn't matter too much, because it was a movie shot the way I told you. But on *Summer Storm*, my next picture, where I had Shuftan again, it did.

Summer Storm *is an adaptation of a Chekhov story?*

This was an old Ufa project. When I was about eleven I went with my father to stay in St Petersburg. I became closely acquainted with Russian literature as a youth. I wanted to do the Chekhov story, *The Shooting Party*, which is Chekhov's only novel, at Ufa, with Willy Birgel in the main part: he had the qualities for it, which I later found in George Sanders, who did the part in America. They both had the same broken identity.

I hired Jimmy Cain for a writer – he was someone I had a very high regard for, particularly for *The Postman Always Rings Twice*. Jimmy Cain was crazy about the treatment and the story, but he Americanized it so much that by the end you'd have thought Chekhov had been writing about Milwaukee. So Jimmy Cain said, 'Let me off the picture. Get another guy.' So then I got Rowland Leigh, a very English Englishman. And we wrote it together. The other name on the credits there, Michael O'Hara, is me. . . . I think they needed another name for the budget, and I'd just read *Appointment in Samarra* by John O'Hara.

I cast Edward Everett Horton in the part of the Count. Everyone told me I was mad, and a lot of pressure was put on me to fire him, but I refused, and I thought he was excellent; he got great reviews.

He is on record saying that this is the best part he ever had, and that you are the best director he ever worked with.

Well, I was very pleased with the casting, because Horton, being cast against type, brought out all the ambiguity of this lousy figure, Count Volsky. The same with the Sanders character, who is a provincial judge. Sanders had lived in Russia, as you may know, and knew Russian. He saw exactly what I was trying to do, and he was the first person to approve the casting of Horton. He himself was just right as the judge. His haughtiness and blasé attitude hiding the rootlessness of the personality . . . this small judge in a small, dirty little town, behaving like the Tsar's brother-in-law: he *has* to get drunk; he *has* to have love affairs. With guys like him and the count going round there had to be a revolution.

In fact you updated it to put the end after the 1917 Revolution, didn't you?

Yes, I did. That way I was able to use the Revolution and the post-revolutionary period to accentuate Chekhov's approach.

The film is constructed within a flashback, which is how the Chekhov original is written as well, isn't it?

Sure. But there is another thing about the flashback I'd just like to mention here. I introduced a change into the Chekhov story, right at the end. After Sanders has mailed off the confession of his corrupt past, being a weak man, he immediately regrets having done this, and tries to get it back again – and there is a great scene there. And this parallels an earlier moment in the film, during the trial, where he also has a momentary impulse towards honesty, which is at once overcome. The flashback tells the story in advance – but not the whole

'With guys like him and the count going round there had to be a revolution': before it, George Sanders (Fedor Petroff) and Edward Everett Horton (Count Volsky) contemplate Linda Darnell (Olga, the peasant girl) (above); and after it, gaze at the memory of their past (*Summer Storm*)

story. I used it to destroy suspense in order to create suspense, a different kind of suspense, or anti-suspense. I don't work well with ordinary suspense. I've always tried to avoid it, and I usually have managed to do so. Or else you have to be a Hitchcock, and then you can do it. I just saw *Topaz* the other day, and I thought it was very good. . . .

I had a lot of things referring to the revolutionary period, the period after the Chekhov story, dialogue, and other things like a picture of Stalin on the wall in the editor's office, which the producers cut out because they were afraid they might not go over well with an American audience. But the flashback was very useful, because in this way I could give a portrayal of post-revolutionary Russia, in contrast to the former story, and show the shoddy judge and the shoddy count, and enhance the contrasts of the piece.

The Chekhov story lent itself very well to the theme that interested me, because he, too, was just showing what social forces were at work. What I tried to do was just to show it how it was. After that it's up to the audience. You don't achieve anything by upsetting people. The properties of the minds of the persons in a picture, or a play, ought to be enigmatized by the writer, or the director, thereby setting in motion the curiosity and emotion of the spectator. The only way of creating suspense, I think, and true participation on the part of an observer is just that. Sometimes in Godard, for example, I think the criticism is too obvious. But a picture I liked a lot recently was *Easy Rider*. You know exactly what the characters want to say. It's obvious, but not because the people in it are sounding-boards. They remain innocent, and the effect is tremendous. I consider it an excellent picture. Your characters have to remain innocent of what your picture is after. They never should step forward. And you must not have caricatures. Ambiguity in technique is important. People shouldn't be what in German is called *eindeutig*.[4] All the contradictions of a character have to be there.

Perhaps I can explain what I mean about my method by reference to two plays which I much admire. One is *Othello*. Othello is a man who has been captured by a stratum of society and made its slave. He has become the slave of the establishment – and this is brilliantly shown in his first speech. He is a character written by Shakespeare at a double level, although the two levels are fused. Or take *El Alcalde de Zalamea* by Calderón: this is interesting in two ways as far as my

70

picture-making is concerned: as a very popular play, and as a piece of tremendous social criticism – Catholicism can be a means of social criticism, too. *El Alcalde de Zalamea* is a play of the utmost audacity, certainly for its time, if not for any. The play runs its uncompromising way down to the end, or almost to it; then, in order to achieve the necessary happy outcome of the goings on, when there is apparently no way out, God steps forward in the person of the king and ties up all the threads, punishes the bad, and pardons the good one, who is the revolutionary. This is done in the crude shocking manner of Euripides. It is the perfect pattern for a melodrama.

At any rate, to come back to *Summer Storm*, the picture was a money-maker, and it got great reviews. And I had a very good time making it; I especially loved working with Sanders.

It's interesting what you say about George Sanders, because the whole Hollywood approach to actors and acting seems aberrant. The greatest actors – John Wayne, Robert Mitchum, Cary Grant – may be given the leads, but they rarely are written about as being the greatest actors. This is all part of the lack, historically, of a real cinema criticism in the States, and in England.

When I came to America I found John Wayne being appreciated as the most wooden and incompetent leading man in pictures. No one ever had a worse press. He was taking one beating after another. In every picture, even if it might be by a great director like Ford or Hawks, he was panned by virtually every critic. I always thought he was a great movie actor, even though I never agreed with his politics. And after only recently seeing him again in a picture I should like to call him an outstanding personage of undiminished power and simplicity – a simplicity not marred by any 'acting' tricks.

Of course, there is always the danger of petrification, of sameness, of not re-shaping your style. Because the only kind of style these actors have at their command is the one of their personality. But don't forget that petrification makes for greatness, sometimes. Petrification leads to being a statue of yourself. Wayne is a great actor because he has become petrified. He has become a statue. You need an *auteur* theory on this, too. Because he has a very consistent

71

handwriting, all his own. I enjoy seeing him: he has become a cipher, a sign in the cinema. Like Charlie Chaplin – he has become a cipher, too. You can't talk about him changing, at least not basically.

Was the situation any better in Germany?

The trouble there was that Berlin was both the movie capital and the theatrical capital of Germany. An actor who the night before might have been doing King Lear was on the set in the morning to do a movie part, and you could still feel the moves, the intonation of the stage. Sometimes I had to spend a whole morning scraping off the staginess.

I found Heinrich George a bit heavy in Pillars of Society.

He was not one of the worst. On the contrary, he was an actor very sensitive to the cinema. He was considered the greatest living German actor on the stage, and he certainly was – although he became a terrific Nazi later. But at least he was very aware of the problem of staginess, and I can remember him asking me fervently to eliminate all possible traces of it in his movie-acting.

The great danger in Germany was the refusal to understand the movies as a new medium, as something worthy of taking its place alongside the stage. Part of the problem I think came in with the talkies. Because the silent actors weren't stage actors. But when the talkies came in, they thought they had to get people from the stage. I think this was a mistake. Actors and directors read too many reviews, just the same as in America, as I found out later – and remember there were no real cinéphiles in those days. The literary critic of the *New York Times* carried disproportionate weight, as did the so-called cinema critics. Today you have an audience of young people who are beginning to become aware of the values of cinema as a new medium independent of traditional aesthetics. That's why I'm so pleased to read a book like Wollen's *Signs and Meaning in the Cinema*, or Sarris's *The American Cinema*: these are something really revolutionary.

Is it right that you were going to do a film called Cagliostro *for Edward Small after* Summer Storm?

That's right. He asked me to do two pictures for him, and one was to be *Cagliostro*. It was based on a novel by Dumas, *Memoirs of a Physician*, and I worked on it for quite a while, and had a complete script ready. I had cast Sanders in the lead as Count Cagliostro, and Akim Tamiroff as his sidekick. Cagliostro was one of those vacillating characters. . . .

So you carried over some of this to A Scandal in Paris, *with the same relationship between George Sanders and Akim Tamiroff?*

That's right. I wrote *A Scandal in Paris* together with Ellis St Joseph, who was a very gifted short story writer, and he did an excellent job on the script.

It's got some great lines.

Well, Sanders delivered them in a truly masterful style. It was a very happy time on this picture. As you know, Vidocq was one of these in-between characters: a crook turned policeman, but still a crook. The starting point was this: if you want to catch a thief, find another thief to do the job. George Sanders had a great capacity for understanding in-between values, being an in-between person himself. He got all the vacillation of the character, its irony. He had just the right degree of arrogance and aplomb for the part. I thought he was great in all the pictures he did with me.

In this film I tried to go beyond realism in the way I presented the story. It became almost surrealist. In the manner of the American surrealists, not the French ones. The picture was not very successful. This was presumably because I adopted a position which brought out the irony, and that doesn't go down well at all with an American audience. This is not a reproach. It is only that American audiences are generally too simple and too naïve – in the best sense of the terms – to be sensitive to irony. They want a cut and dried stance, for or against. But the nuances which handle both at the same time and make Europeans smile are completely foreign to Americans. This is why some of Shakespeare's plays like *Troilus and Cressida* have never been successful in the States.

But, of course, I only showed a small part of Vidocq's life in the picture. You could have made a whole series of films out of his life –

like about Cagliostro – as well. But the part I used is the most interesting period, it lends itself best to irony – there is a lot of it in the cop–thief oscillation. And this gives the Sanders character plenty of space to operate in.

Hanns Eisler has a credit for the music: how come you chose him, and how do you feel about his music on the film? He was a pupil of Schoenberg's, wasn't he?[5]

That's right. Well, he was a good friend and a good guy, apart from being an excellent musician. Eisler felt it hadn't quite come off. I think there are still moments of great music in the picture, but Eisler became aware of a heavy-handedness in his composer's touch, which was wrong for this picture and since, as always in the movies, time was pressing and the picture had to go into release, he gave up, feeling he would have to start anew on the score. I still regret that this was made impossible by the circumstances.

Did you have any trouble because of working with him? He was the main person the House Un-American Activities Committee dragged up with Brecht, wasn't he?

Yes, he was. But I didn't have any trouble because of him.

Lured *is alleged to be a re-make of Siodmak's* Pièges: *is that right?*

Well, I don't think I ever saw that. Rostén had a treatment on an old script, which was set in Paris, and so I suppose this was the Siodmak.

Lured *is a very weird film, with an extraordinary cast: did you have a relatively free hand on it?*

Yes, I did. I got on well with Hunt Stromberg, the producer. He liked my direction, and he gave me a very free hand, on the cutting and everything. I also had a great art director on this picture – Remisoff, a Russian. He did an expert job. And this was also the first time I worked with Bill Daniels, a very good cameraman.

The cast was right. I tried with Karloff to do something like I had done with Horton in *Summer Storm*, and Karloff was very pleased with the role. It was a bit the same with Coburn, who was considered a comedy actor, and this gave the part of the detective an added quality, with his bonhomie. Lucille Ball, too, was known as a comedy actress. Here, you remember, she hires herself to the police as an under-cover agent, and I think I got some irony into the character, and some of the shifting identity I had in the Vidocq and Cagliostro characters: all three of them seem to others to be something different from what they really are. In the casting I was operating on a two-layer principle. And it was my first attempt at a crime picture. In many ways, in style and theme, it was a continuation of the Cagliostro and Vidocq pictures.

You know it came out in England called Personal Column?

Indeed I do. They changed the title during the run in America as well. *Lured* was a great title, it has a sound to it. The picture had been doing very well, and the change ruined the run. *Personal Column* sounds like Hedda Hopper to me. Stromberg wanted something 'more dignified'.

Can you tell me about Sleep, My Love? *I must admit that when I watched it I was puzzled as to how and why you'd made it.*

The only thing I was interested in was the Claudette Colbert part (Alison Courtland), because of the way the plot was constructed. There was nothing else I could do.

What is the position about Siren of Atlantis, *part of which you are credited with having shot?*

I'm fairly sure I didn't do any shooting on this. But I may have done some writing. . . . I think I did some work on the screenplay with Rowland Leigh.

How did it come up?

Rudi Joseph came to me and asked me if I wanted to do the picture, *Atlantis* – Rudi had been an assistant to Pabst. And

75

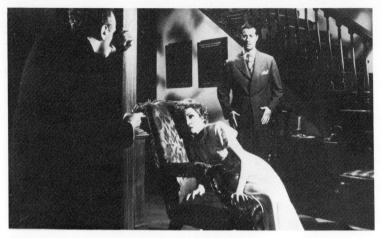

Sleep, My Love: the fake psychiatrist, George Coulouris, turns on the man who has hired him (Don Ameche) to kill his wife (Claudette Colbert)

Nebenzal, who owned the picture, asked me if I would re-write the story. I said I'd try, but I wouldn't direct it.

Why didn't you want to shoot it?

First, because the Pabst film was a very good film. The best thing to do, as I told Nebenzal, was just to re-release the Pabst, but he (Nebenzal) didn't want to do that. And, besides, he didn't have the money to do the necessary fantastic sets. You know, *Atlantis* depends on inspiring people's fantasies. The old Pabst picture had great sets, but you do need money to construct a hidden city and that kind of thing. It's no good trying to shoot this sort of film on a small budget, as Nebenzal wanted – and then he wanted me to use some of the long-shot material from the old Pabst, and so on.

I think what happened then is that after I'd said I wouldn't direct it, Nebenzal got in Ripley, and he shot it, and for various reasons not to do with Ripley, but mainly with the cast, it did not come off. And then Nebenzal asked me to 'salvage' it, but I didn't want to have anything to do with it any more.

I just saw it by chance, and it had some things in it: the flashback construction, the chess, and some particular shots I thought might have been yours.

Well, perhaps the chess I wrote into the script.

You're also credited in some sources with work – and even direction – on Lulu Belle.

I think I perhaps did some writing on this, but I don't think I did any shooting. I remember I worked on three pictures at Columbia: two were certainly *Shockproof* and *Slightly French*, so maybe this was the third, but I don't know for sure.

Can you tell me anything about Slightly French, *the film you made about Hollywood?*

I can't. I have no feeling for this picture at all.

So it can't be taken as any kind of comment by you on the Hollywood scene?

No. I had no freedom on it at all.

What happened on Shockproof?

I don't remember it all too well. But I do recall that Fuller – whom I never met – brought a script to Columbia, which I was supposed to shoot. I liked the script tremendously. But, against my wish, they called in Helen Deutsch to change it. I had no influence on the script myself, especially since Helen Deutsch turned herself into the co-producer, I think, presumably to institutionalize her control.

As you may know, the original title was *The Lovers*, and there was something great in Fuller's ending, which was then changed by Helen Deutsch and Columbia, which I think was a shame. There was something gutty in Fuller's original script. The character of the cop was interesting. He fell in love. He left his job. He hid. And then it ended with him shooting it out with the other policeman. Cop against cop. It was very melodramatic, of course, but in between the battle sequences there were situations of love. Love that cannot be fulfilled. Love in extreme circumstances, love socially conditioned ... and impossible. In Fuller's ending the guy had changed. Something had started blooming in that goddam cop's soul.

Now, there is something rather strange I would like to tell you about this picture, though this may be deviating a bit. In looking back, I feel there is a certain pattern evident in recurrent phases of my play- and picture-making. And *Shockproof*, which is a very minor picture of mine, and not one that is in any sense my own, is maybe a good occasion to say something about this, because it ties up with two theatrical events in my past. One is *The Silver Lake*, by Kaiser and Weill, which I've told you about. Now, in this Kaiser had a basic situation rather like the one in Fuller's script, or at least there were similarities. Kaiser put the cop as the instrument of society, and Fuller's story at least could have been like this: it could have been a piece of digging into social circumstances.

But there's another tie-up, with another play, *Faith, Love, Hope* — which is an ironic biblical reference equivalent in German to the English 'love, hope, charity'.[6] I was taken to see this play in a little off-theatre in Vienna in November 1936 by Max Brod, Kafka's friend. Werfel was there, and so was my friend Csokor, a then very important playwright.[7] The play was by Odön von Horvath, then a little-known author, except to a narrow circle of ardent admirers. In recent years his work, which mainly consists of plays, has gained recognition as that of one of the best dramatists of his generation, and some people rank his name alongside that of Brecht.[8] I liked his play a lot. His characters, in their brooding poetry, captivate if not the mind, the deeper and more archaic essence of the spectator's being. ... Now, this play had practically the same theme as Fuller's script: the cop and a girl just released from prison, their love. A different ending, though. Because in Horvath's darkly existing Viennese world, there is no place for the pathos of true love. Love just licks and ripples round the lonesome rock of the human condition. At any rate, I was impressed by the picture possibilities of Horvath's play. I suggested it to Ufa, even wrote a treatment. But ultimately the project was turned down by the front office, because of its inherent social and political implications.

Without any doubt, one could have made something similar out of *Shockproof*, it could have been such a piece of critique. But the studio's revisions most consciously avoided and detoured any story elements which pointed in this direction.[9]

What do you make of Richard Hamilton's paintings based on the still from Shockproof?[10]

I've been looking at the catalogue. There is a wonderful clarity in Hamilton's work. And looking at these pictures some things have come back to me – Pat Knight's rather angular handsomeness, the pale lipstick face, with eyes trying to hide something, and an attitude of sameness about her against the changing backgrounds and melodramatic action. She was not enormously talented as an actress, but I decided to use this very lack of experience – and she was most flexible and willing and kind of understood what I was after – the sparse freedom of human existence.

And there is another thing: what Richard Hamilton says there about the drawer in the still of Pat Knight illustrates very well a point about my style.[11] The open drawer, which Hamilton has picked out, is pointing to the woman and running out of shot. A fragment running out of shot puts the observer into the picture in a way. The moment you have the whole table and drawer there you just become a voyeur. This ties up with the placing of fragments of objects which I discovered for the first time with *Pillars of Society*. The point is there is no such thing as a dead thing and a live thing.

Hence the role of statues and mirrors in your movies, objects which are intermediate?

Yes, although one mustn't be seduced. . . . After this picture I was completely fed up with Harry Cohn and really sick of the whole business. So I went back to Europe for almost a year – this must have been 1949–50. We don't have to go into this, but everything went wrong. The whole movie situation was catastrophic. Ufa had been dissolved by the Americans, and I think this was stupid. It certainly contributed to the wrecking of the German cinema, and the effects are still being felt.

But, anyway, after this German experience, I came back to the States feeling very demoralized. You know, the Germans were *blaming* you for leaving when the Nazis were in power – just as they have attacked Willy Brandt for the same thing, and he was one of the few

79

Painting by Richard Hamilton based on a still from *Shockproof*, with Patricia Knight

guys with the guts to prefer an uncertain future to the Nazified fatherland.

But I'd like to tell you a story, which I find rather significant, and it concerns a play by Zuckmayer, whom I've talked about already. Zuckmayer was the only emigrant who was welcomed back to Germany with open arms, I would say. Partly because he had written a play in America called *The Devil's General* (*Des Teufels General*) which was incredibly successful in Germany.[12] It was interpreted by the Germans as being definitely pro-German, although certainly not meant so by Zuckmayer. The hero of the play is a Nazi general, who is a good Nazi. And I think the play was such a huge success because it allowed the Germans to see a Nazi (because this general was wearing Nazi uniform), and to be able to express their feelings towards Nazism, which were sympathetic, in a context where they did not have to be explicit. They could applaud the play when, I feel, they were really applauding the Nazis. And when I saw the play, after the last curtain the crowd surged forward in the theatre and chaired the hero off the stage in his Nazi uniform and out into the streets. And in the streets people joined in the procession when they saw this triumphant Nazi uniform on the shoulders of the audience.

1. It was made into a film by Jack Clayton in 1961 (*The Innocents*).
2. Filmed by Tony Richardson in 1969.
3. Ludwig was a best-selling author, famous for numerous biographies – of Lincoln, Masaryk, Bismarck, and others. He also conducted an extremely penetrating interview with Stalin. Sirk had staged a couple of Ludwig's plays at Chemnitz.
4. Literally: 'with only one meaning'.
5. Hanns Eisler (1898–1962) is the author of one of the few outstanding marxist books on the arts, *Composing for the Films*, London, 1951. He wrote the music for the Comintern song (with words by Mayakovsky). He also worked for many years with Brecht, and did the music for several films, including *Hangmen Also Die* (Fritz Lang) and *Woman on the Beach* (Renoir). He was the brother of Gerhart Eisler and Ruth Fischer.
6. The play is titled *Glaube Liebe Hoffnung: Ein Kleiner Totentanz*, although when originally staged, it was called *Liebe Pflicht und Hoffnung* (*Love, Duty and Hope*).
7. Franz Werfel (1890–1945) was one of the most extraordinary figures in twentieth-century German culture. Originally a leading Expressionist, author of *Nicht der Mörder, der ermordete ist Schuldig* (*Not the Murderer, but the Murdered Man is Guilty*) and *Spiegelmensch* (*Mirror Man*) 1920, he ended up writing *The Song of Bernadette* in Beverly Hills, after passing through Lourdes in his flight from the Nazis. Franz Theodor Csokor was an Austrian playwright, best known for his *3 November 1918*, a play about the last days of the Austro-Hungarian army, just before it disintegrated into its different national components.
8. 'Horvath, who became an emigrant later on, died a strange death in Paris two years later. Just opposite the Théâtre de Marigny, on the Champs-Elysées, he was killed by a falling tree'. He was en route to see Robert Siodmak.
9. For Fuller on the script, see *Samuel Fuller* ed. David Will and Peter Wollen, Edinburgh, 1969, pp. 98–9.
10. *Catalogue* of Richard Hamilton Exhibition, the Tate Gallery, London, 1970. Richard Hamilton has done a series of paintings based on, or inspired by, a still of Patricia Knight in *Shockproof*.
11. 'A collection of quite different images attain a common identity by the way they contribute to a group. I tried to provide the same type of elements in each version though they are not identical. A curtain (so much in the foreground that it puts the spectator outside the interior) helps to make the spectator's position illicit – a Peeping Tom: this is another reason why the camera must not be felt by the occupant. . . . There is a compositional unity in that the figure is placed at the visual centre. The carpet (or desk) acts like an arrow in directing attention. Although there is no consistent vanishing point there is a persistent tendency for lines to converge on the figure. In the *Shockproof* still the desk partly hides the body of a man Patricia Knight has just killed in a struggle for a gun. The dramatic role of the dead man is transferred to the lurid colour treatment of the carpet.' (Richard Hamilton, *Catalogue*, pp. 51–2.)
12. Since made into a film by Helmet Käutner (1955).

81

5: America II: 1950–1959

So after this I went back to Hollywood.

Was your contract with Columbia expired by now?

No, it had been cancelled when I left to go back to Germany. One of the people I went to see when I returned to America was Nebenzal, and he offered me a picture: it was a re-make of *M*. I said, 'Why don't you get Lang to do it?' Nebenzal said he'd had a lot of trouble with Lang on the original, which he (Nebenzal) had produced back in Germany. I turned it down.

Why?

I felt I shouldn't make the picture if Lang didn't want to do it, quite apart from not wanting to re-make someone else's work, particularly when it was good. What I said was: let's do a *new* story of a *new* sex pervert, with George Sanders in the lead part. I worked on a new script for a while, but Nebenzal still remained fond of the old idea, he wanted to re-make the old picture. And then I believe it was made by Losey.[1]

Among other people I went round to see were Rudi Joseph and Brettauer. And in Brettauer's office I met Boyer. We got talking. He was disgusted with his recent picture, *Arch of Triumph*,[2] and he badly needed to move on to something entirely new to get his career going again. Now, it had been suggested earlier I should do a film out of the play *First Legion* by Lavery. Boyer liked the idea very much, and he had a couple of my pictures screened – *Summer Storm* and *Lured* – and he liked them. So we agreed to do the picture, as an independent production. I think originally Boyer was going to produce it, but then he told me he'd prefer me to produce it, which I did in the end with Rudi Joseph.

We made it on a rather small budget. It was shot entirely on location, mainly at the Mission Inn, Riverside. Many of the rooms were very small, just tiny cells, and I had to use a deep-focus lens all the time to get the shots, because by the time you had all the lighting equipment and a few technicians in there there was hardly any room left for the actors. Technically, the picture was interesting to me because of its being completely away from the studio. Where and how you shoot a film is a technical matter, but it is also something wider than that: it is integral to its whole conception; it gives an unmistakable character to the picture.

I've never seen it, but the stills make it look as though you got some good casting.

That's right. There were some excellent actors in it. I wanted to do something like I did on *Summer Storm*, cast it against type. I wanted the picture to be very ironical – but I've never seen it since, and I don't know if it comes off. What I was trying to do was to push it definitely towards comedy. There is a miracle that is not a miracle, but because of it a lot of things happen to this little monastery, and then God says, 'Now I'll send them a real miracle.' It is as if God is stepping forward saying, 'It seems there has been a false miracle around here, a thing which can make no one very happy, but by God there shall be a real one. I'll show you,' and he rolls up his sleeves.

It was quite a success with the critics. But the Jesuit fathers who were there had to give the OK on everything. They were on the set the whole time, scrutinizing every line and implication. You'd get something okayed, and then one of them would say, 'But you *could* interpret this as anti-religious,' or something. I think it could have been a sharper picture, more clearly in focus, if they hadn't been there.

Why are you so interested in religion? Why does it figure so prominently in many of your films?

Religion – or sorcery? Charles Boyer (left), and Lyle Bettger as the agnostic doctor with Barbara Rush in *The First Legion*

That is a bit hard to answer. But, basically, let me say this: I see religion as a very important part of bourgeois society. It is a pillar of this society, if a broken pillar. The marble is showing quite a bit of decay. If you want to make pictures about this society, I think it is an ingredient of a bygone charm – charm in the original sense of the word: sorcery.

I've always been interested in religion, even though I haven't been to church for decades. It is one of my constant preoccupations. Even not believing in God is a religious act in a way. All the great classical plays have religious subjects, to some extent. I wanted to stage Euripides's *Bacchae* once: this is a very modern play, and by far his best as far as I am concerned. It is all about religion and sex. And I wrote a play about religion myself, but I wasn't entirely happy with it. You know, in a way, I think everything is about religion: it's about the unknown things in man.

In my thirties I read two books which had a certain influence on my approach to religion: Gilbert Murray's *Five Stages of Greek Religion* and Jane Ellen Harrison's *Themis: A Study of the Social Origins of Religion*. Both books postulate, as Harrison puts it, that God and gods and religious ideas reflect the social activities of the worshipper. In the meantime, of course, this has become a generally accepted idea. *The First Legion*, relating religion and the absurd (the miracle) is to be understood in this way. And so, later on, is *Battle*

Hymn, which deals with the relationship between religion and war. But also *Sign of the Pagan* and *Thunder on the Hill*, and there are traces in *Imitation of Life*. This would also go for several plays I put on in Germany earlier, like *Berenga*, *Oedipus Rex*, *Saint Joan*, and Johst's *The Prophets*, and others.

Religion figures most prominently in your next movie, Thunder on the Hill, *too.*

Yes, but I wanted this picture to have *nothing* to do with religion. For me, there is one interesting theme in it: this girl (Ann Blyth) being taken to the gallows, the storm, the delay, and so on. This should have been the only thing the picture was about. There was no story in the Claudette Colbert part (Sister Bonaventure).

But it was not my next picture after *The First Legion*: the filmography is not correct here. I made *The First Legion* when I came back to America, then I next made *Mystery Submarine* for Universal, and then after that *Thunder on the Hill*.

How did you come to sign up with Universal?

Back in the Columbia days I got several offers from studios, all of which I had to turn down because Harry Cohn wouldn't release me. I think it was in 1946, after Universal had seen *A Scandal in Paris* they offered me a contract. After my picture with Boyer, I remembered this and went back to see them and ask them if they were still interested. And so they said, 'Yes, but we'd have to sign you for a seven-year contract.' I said, 'OK, I'll sign, on condition you guarantee me one A-picture' – and this was to be *Thunder on the Hill*, which was based on an English play, *Bonaventure*.

And from then on you stayed with Universal?

I did. They were a smaller studio than Columbia. But they were most decent to me. I'd like to go on the record with that.

I became a kind of house director of Universal. Conditions were not perfect, but when I complained about a story, they would say to me, 'If you can get a star, great; you can have more money and pick a better story.' But at least I was allowed to work on the material – so that I restructured to some extent some of the rather impossible scripts of the films I had to direct. Of course, I had to go by the rules, avoid experiments, stick to family fare, have 'happy endings', and so on.

Universal didn't interfere with either my camerawork or my cutting – which meant a lot to me. In a way, I did see their point of view, running a studio: a film has to make back its money. I think all the best directors would agree with me about that – Ford, Hawks, or Hitchcock certainly would. There has never been a time in showbusiness, going back to Calderón, Shakespeare, Lope de Vega, Molière, when this hasn't been the case. I think if Shakespeare were alive today he'd shake me by the hand and say, 'My dear boy, I know what it was like in Hollywood. I had to make money, too, and a lot of my stories were lousy' – which they were. Shakespeare put himself into his sonnets, but some of his plays were not so good. . . .

The only one of these early Universal films I've seen is Has Anybody Seen My Gal? *– which I liked.*

I can't remember it too well. I have a painter's memory, not a memory for stories. I can remember where I was interested in something, or trying to do something that was my own. But not where I had stories so bad that all I could do was try and overcome them.

Has Anybody Seen My Gal? *was Rock Hudson's first picture with you, wasn't it?*

Yes, it was.

How did you come to make so many films with him?

Well, there had emerged a kind of B-picture creation at Universal against the trend of the time, as I thought, and as I was proven right later. This was partly caused by the lack of house-owned stars. The only thing to do in these circumstances was to manufacture a star, because getting more money depended on having a name in your picture. So I looked around, and I saw a picture Rock was playing in, with Chandler in the lead (*Iron Man*).[3] He had a small part, and he was far inferior to Chandler, but I thought I saw something. So I arranged to meet him, and he seemed to be not too much to the eye, except very handsome. But the camera sees with its own eye. It sees things the human eye does not detect. And ultimately you learn to trust your camera. I gave him an extensive test, and then I put him into *Has Anybody Seen My Gal?* The only thing which never let me down in Hollywood was my camera. And it was not wrong about Hudson. Within a very few years he became a number one box-office star in America.

You also had James Dean in the film, and I thought he was good: what happened after that?

He just disappeared. I think they must have terminated his contract. But I thought he was fine in the part, too.

You know, the only one of the early Universal pictures which has a place in my memory was the Ann Sheridan one (*Take Me To Town*). I had the idea of doing a trilogy of little American stories, which was supposed to be *Has Anybody Seen My Gal?*, *Meet Me At the Fair*, and *Take Me To Town*.

Can you remember anything about Meet Me At The Fair*?*

Well, it was again a kind of period picture, like *Has Anybody Seen My Gal?* Irving Wallace wrote the script. He wasn't yet well known, but he was just writing the novel which was to give him a best-seller name. What I had in mind here was another piece of Americana, too: it's a colour picture. It's a story about a boy in an orphanage who gets tied up with a couple of show people, going to fairs. One of them was a Negro, which interested me, and the other guy was Dan Dailey. It's a kind of small-town political picture as well: it's about crooked politicians, who are diverting funds from the orphanage, and who are eventually uncovered by the show-business people and the boy.

Dan Dailey's a good actor. You don't sound too happy about the film – what didn't work out?

I think the music was not good enough. For such a picture you need a couple of fresh hits. Dan Dailey was good. He even, I thought, had some elements of Sanders's way of acting in his performance: cool, a little cynical, selling his medicines which at the same time caused and cured diarrhoea; he maintained a nice and merry pace throughout the little exciting story by Gene Markey, one of the highest-paid writers in Hollywood. But Dan could do very little with the material.

I tried at least to do a little more. But I don't have the feeling that I fully succeeded. And then there was the title. I objected to it, mainly because it was, I think, derived from *Meet Me In St Louis*, and you were challenged to compare it to that extremely successful, super-A production with Judy Garland and a splendid cast, and splendid music.

For your next film, Take Me To Town, *you had Russell Metty as the cameraman for the first time.*

That's right. And we did about ten pictures together afterwards.

How did you get to work with him?

I saw some pictures he had done, and I asked Universal to get him. He was very expensive, and very much in demand, but I finally succeeded. We always agreed about everything: we had just the same way of seeing things, and we had a great time working together. I liked working with a group of people I knew well, and he was the main one in this group. I am sure this way of working with a group stems from the theatre, where I always had my own troupe.

I have a very happy memory of this picture. It was a little lyrical poem to the American Western past. It's about a saloon-girl and a preacher. I had Sterling Hayden and Ann Sheridan. She was the star, and I liked working with her. She had real presence, a wonderful glow. And there was some sadness about her, underlying the gaiety of the part, which I think enhanced her performance to a discriminating eye. At any rate, I thought in this little picture she was at the same time less and more than she had been before. She maybe had lost in sex-appeal, and gained in a human one. This movie was something of a farewell to cinema for her.

As I told you, *Take Me To Town* was supposed to be part of a larger idea I had – a group of stories about small-town life. I felt that with the little money at my disposal it was best to stick to relatively modest projects. And the next picture also, in a way, falls into the same group. This was *Stopover*, released under the title *All I Desire*, a title change I did not like, for reasons pertaining to the whole conception of the story – but let's come to that later. I wanted to do all these pictures in colour – which I considered very essential to this type of picture to give it the necessary warmth and glow and, commercially, to add box-office power to their rather second-rate star value – but the studio wouldn't give me colour for it.

Why not, since they'd given it to you for the previous three?

That's because they were all musicals, of a kind – and for a musical colour was considered essential.

Wasn't Barbara Stanwyck a big enough star to raise money on for the film?

I don't think she was any more – though she was an excellent actress, I might add: one of the best in town. In this picture she had the unsentimental sadness of a broken life about her. This was a pre-study of the 'actress' in *Imitation of Life*. She comes back from an imitated life. ... I was attracted by the title, *Stopover*. Stanwyck doesn't get into her love again – there is something blocking her. A woman comes back with all her dreams, with her love – and she finds nothing but this rotten, decrepit middle-class American family.

In the book Naomi (Barbara Stanwyck) leaves: it is only a stopover. In the film she stays.

Well, that's the 'happy end', so-called. Ross Hunter was iron. We had to have it. But that was a further reason I wanted to keep *Stopover* as the title for the picture. It was a much darker title. It would have deepened the picture and the character – and at the same time the irony.

Why did you change the play that is staged in the story from The Rivals *to* Baroness Barclay's Secret?

I wanted to keep it small. This was just a slice of life, you know, not all of life itself. If I'd kept *The Rivals*, it would have opened up a can of beans. I would have found it very hard to do this without let-

Take Me to Town: Sterling Hayden as the preacher in the river

ting it run away with me. I know *The Rivals* is standard small town fare, but that's only part of it – the rest of the problem concerns myself.

I was quite surprised after these pieces of Americana to find you turning to quite another kind of American film – a Western, Taza.

I wanted to do a Western. And after *Has Anybody Seen My Gal?* Hudson wanted to work with me again, and so we did this picture with him as an Indian. He wanted to do the part, although the studio weren't keen on him doing an Indian again, because he'd just done an Indian, and they thought it might spoil his image – you know these problems about actors doing Indians too often. And Hudson was new, he wasn't a star yet. But he wanted to do it, and he wanted to work with me.

So I was delighted to get out into the desert and among the Indians: this was my main reason for doing the picture. I was very interested in the Indians, and I tried to get plenty of lore into the picture. It was shot entirely in Utah, mostly near Moab, and a bit

90

'A woman comes back with all her dreams, with her love – and she finds nothing but this rotten, decrepit, middle-class American family': Barbara Stanwyck (centre) with Richard Carlson, Lori Nelson, Marcia Henderson and Lotte Stein in *All I Desire*. *Cf.* the still on page 106 (*There's Always Tomorrow*)

above the Upper Colorado. It was shot completely outdoors, and improvised. There are a few sets, but they were all built there, on the spot – by the Indians, too. And they were real Indians in the picture, they hadn't been spoiled by Ford. I had a big battle in the picture where they really started fighting like hell. None of them could speak English, and we had a couple of interpreters for the two tribes of Apaches – who couldn't speak each others' language either. The battle was one of the most exciting things I've ever done. It took a week, and I shot it with four cameras. It was, technically, the most difficult thing I think I have ever done. And here I had Metty again, and he did a very good job under extreme circumstances – because it was mid-summer, and hot as hell.

This was the first time I had George Zuckerman working with me. We did the script together; he was an excellent writer, I think. And together we built Hudson one of those intermediate parts.

He goes round in that very symbolic gear – half Indian gear, half policeman.

Rock Hudson as *Taza, Son of Cochise*

That's right. He is my most symbolic in-between man. He is an Indian, but there has seeped into the character this element of civilization. . . . I think the picture catches the lyricism of the Indian love affair, the grasping for words, the great shyness. And Barbara Rush was excellent as the girl.

I stuck in the Chandler funeral at the beginning – though Chandler didn't want to do it. He had done Cochise already, which was the whole point. When I suggested it to him, he said, 'But, my God, I'm a star! . . . Just to do five minutes and then die!' But I needed Chandler to start it off, and I think this also contributed to a change in the title. Before Chandler came in – for a large sum of money – it had a different title.

Was shooting the film in 3D a help or a hindrance?

It was no help. It was just an experiment. You remember, it was a time of a certain technical revolution, the wide screen, etc. Ultimately, the exhibitors didn't like it, so it was scrapped. But it was no help to me.

After that you made Magnificent Obsession, *which is quite another kind of movie, and I'm rather perplexed how you came to make something like this, which is an out-and-out melodrama, to put it mildly.*

Well, first let me tell you how the picture came up, and then I'll try and tell you what I wanted to do with it. Ross Hunter came to me and said, 'I have Jane Wyman.' And I said, 'Oh.' She was still a real star then – and I was terribly interested. He told me: she is interested in a certain story; it's a remake of an old Universal picture that did rather well. . . . The point is there was always this actress remembering the picture. Ross Hunter gave me the book and I tried to read it, but I just couldn't. It is the most confused book you can imagine, it is so abstract in many respects that I didn't see a picture in it. Then he showed me an outline he had had done on the old picture by John Stahl – a name which did not mean anything to me. (And, by the way, I did not see the Stahl picture.) I took the treatment home, and I read it. So far as I remember, the outline was quite different from the book. I had the feeling this could make a picture, but I said to Ross, 'Look, we'll be buried under this thing.' And I went home and wandered round the house in a deep depression for a couple of days, and then, thinking it over, I realized that maybe Jane Wyman could be right and this goddam awful story could be a success. And it was; it topped the receipts of the old Stahl picture by more than ten times, it was Universal's most successful enterprise for years.

Your success with the most unlikely material is very striking: do you think that in fact a certain kind of film about modern America, about things that are important in the society, can only be made in the form of melodrama, if you're working there?

Well, the word 'melodrama' has rather lost its meaning nowadays: people tend to lose the 'melos' in it, the music. I am not an American, indeed I came to this folklore of American melodrama from a world crazily removed from it. But I was always fascinated with the kind of picture which is called a melodrama, in America.

As I told you, at Ufa, I made several pictures which could be called melodramas: *Schlussakkord* was one kind of melodrama; and *Zu Neuen Ufern* and *La Habanera* were another kind of melodrama. But all three were melodramas in the sense of music + drama. Melodrama in the American sense is rather the archetype of a kind of cinema which connects with drama. Most great plays are based on melodrama situations, or have melodramatic endings: *Richard III*, for example, is practically a melodrama. Aeschylus and Sophocles

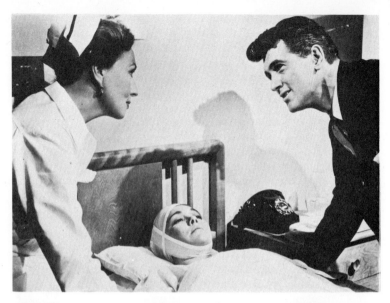

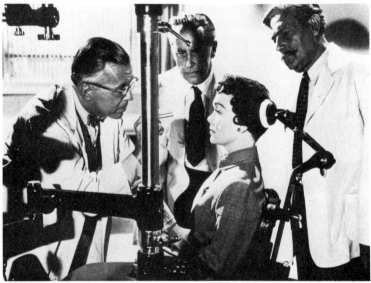

Magnificent Obsession: Rock Hudson with Agnes Moorhead and Jane Wyman, whose sight he has just restored through a brain operation (above); and Jane Wyman surrounded by Zurich doctors

wrote plenty of melodramas, as well. . . . The *Oresteia* is really a melodrama, I think. But what used to take place in the world of kings and princes has since been transposed into the world of the bourgeoisie. Yet the plots remain profoundly similar. There is melodrama in a novelist like Faulkner, for instance.

I am intrigued by the playfulness, and the insincerity, of men. I think often of the connection between 'play' and 'please'. They are the same thing: a play must please. And, in a way, the American melodrama allowed me to do this.

There is one other thing about *Magnificent Obsession*: I was still working on turning Hudson into a star. Now this meant the first occasion for him to ride into stardom on the name of Jane Wyman. This put him on the map. The picture was an enormous success for both him and Jane Wyman – and that's why the studio wanted to make *All That Heaven Allows* right afterwards.

But how do you set about transforming something like the story of Magnificent Obsession *or, later,* Imitation of Life, *for that matter? Because it is much more extraordinary than your success with stories you like, the Faulkner or the Chekhov. Can you pick out the elements which got you going?*

You have to do your utmost to hate it – and to love it. My immediate reaction to *Magnificent Obsession* was bewilderment and discouragement. But still I was attracted by something irrational in it. Something mad, in a way – well, obsessed, because this is a damned crazy story if ever there was one. The blindness of the woman. The irony of it all – not irony in the usual sense of the word, but as a structural element, an element of antinomy. This saintly woman's husband, Dr Phillips, dies so another can live. It is a Euripidean irony – the theme of *Alcestis*: one person pacifying death by taking the place of another. Let me just refresh your memory about the play: a king is to die; his wife, Alcestis, who loves him very much, offers herself instead. Death is satisfied. The husband hesitates. If he accepts he is ruined. If he doesn't he is dead. It is an impossible situation – there is no way out, and Euripides drives it right up to the hilt, and then the god steps out of his machine, just like that, and straightens it all out. What would you do if you were the man? Would you say: 'No, no, I'll die, I'll go back to my place and die instead of you?' or not? I like both the love, and the impossibility. And this is perhaps what I got into *Magnificent Obsession*, although the irony is a bit buried, and the 'happy end' is a little bit more than just a *deus ex machina*. But there is plenty of irony there, just below the surface. . . . Aeschylus and Sophocles were still too pious to handle the problem as freshly as Euripides did. He knew what he was up against, and he solved the apparent contradiction between an impossible situation and the need for a happy end.

And there is another important thing, when I say you have to hate it and love it. Unlike stage directing, where you rehearse in continuity – meaning you are not allowed for a moment to forget the totality of the play – in pictures it is quite different. You shoot completely out of continuity. It is a technical medium, much more than the stage is. You shoot scene No. 8, and maybe only half of it. You go to 126, just take the long shot, which is 5,000 miles away from the studio, come back to the scene after weeks, then finish scene No. 8, and continue in this bewildering way. The matching of the mood of scene and characters, of light and length: all this has to be present at all times in one man's mind – the director's. He is the architect as well as the mason. And being a mason, a good mason, he has a chance to fall in love with each piece of brick, of well-mixed mortar, of the detail. He can like immensely a scene about which he formerly had many reservations, even hostile reservations. At any rate, this maybe incompetent imagery may explain to you what I mean by loving and hating at the same time. If I had had to stage *Magnificent Obsession* as a play I wouldn't have survived. It is a combination of kitsch, and craziness, and trashiness. But craziness is very important, and it saves trashy stuff like *Magnificent Obsession*. This is the dialectic – there is a very short distance between high art and trash, and trash that contains the element of craziness is by this very quality nearer to art.

But there is an internal balance in Magnificent Obsession *between the blindness of Jane Wyman and the false identity of Hudson, so the film has a structure, with contrasting characters, which heightens the impact.*

In almost all my movies, where I had a hand in building the story, there is a kind of solid structure to the picture. You don't always conquer your material, and I can't pretend I always did, because I didn't. . . . But one of the foremost things of picture-making, I think, is to bend your material to your style and your purpose. A director is really a story-bender. This goes together with what I was saying about stories not being 'all-important. A story nearly always leaves you a chance to express something beyond plot or literary values. Look at a few stories – take the famous ones: take *Anna Karenina* by Clarence Brown, with Garbo; take *Camille*, with Garbo, and Cukor directing. Two stories of definitely different literary values. *Camille* a rather cheap one; the other with the mighty breadth and word-power of Tolstoy. But as movies they are not unequal. Take Melville's *Moby Dick* and contrast it with *La Règle du Jeu*. The stories are far from equal, but as pictures I think the scales are in favour of *La Règle du Jeu*. The minor story is by far the better movie material – and heaven knows I'm an admirer of Melville, the greatest in American literature, I think. Even in plays it's not the story that is important: if you think of all the silly plots Shakespeare had, and compare him with Walter Scott . . . it's language that counts. Now, the place of language in pictures has to be taken by the camera – and by cutting. You have to write with the camera.

The theme of blindness, which is in Shockproof *and in the Nabokov project* (Laughter in the Dark) *is most explicit in* Magnificent Obsession.

Sure. I have always been intrigued by the problems of blindness. It was one of the attractions of the Nabokov. And one of my dearest projects was to make a picture set in a blind people's home. There would just have been people ceaselessly tapping, trying to grasp things they could not see. What I think would be extremely interesting here would be to try and confront problems of this kind via a medium – the cinema – which itself is only concerned with things seen. It is this contrast between a world where words have only a limited importance and another world where they are nearly everything that inspires my passionate interest. It is a highly dramatic division. I did in fact write a screenplay on the subject for Columbia, but it never got made into a picture.

In some ways, the most successful of your melodramas, I think, is the follow-on picture, All That Heaven Allows. *This has a very straightforward antithesis between one vacillating character (Jane Wyman) and one very stable and direct one (Rock Hudson).*

True. Because in melodrama it's of advantage to have one immovable character against which you can put your more split ones. Because your audience needs – or likes – to have a character in the movie they can identify themselves with: naturally, the steadfast one, not to be moved. Now, this character preferably ought to be the hero of the story – then it's Gary Cooper, John Wayne, and so on. Or Rock Hudson, as you say. You couldn't make a split character out of Wayne if you tried. I couldn't out of Rock Hudson.

Or the supporting part in the picture is your hidden leading man. Examples: Palance in *Sign of the Pagan*; and almost paradigmatically so in *Written on the Wind*, where again Rock Hudson is the immovable one, the nice guy, but Stack and Malone are the secret owners of the picture.

You can't make a film out of just any kind of character. They aren't all interesting – and even to be interesting is not enough. You do also need balance and antithesis. In *Written on the Wind* I think I hit a fair balance, because you had the interesting characters, Stack and Malone, both brilliantly acted – and you had the counter-balance with Hudson and Bacall, being rather normal and not split within themselves. I think quite a few of my more successful pictures had the same kind of equilibrium. You'll certainly find it in *The Tarnished Angels*. It is there in *Imitation of Life*: the Lana Turner character and Gavin contrasted to the split and restless Susan Kohner. I could go on like this, mentioning, as I think I have done, *Summer Storm*, *All That Heaven Allows*, *Sign of the Pagan*, and others.

I much admired your use of elements like embarrassment in All That Heaven Allows. *I thought the way you used it resumed very well a whole range of social relations – and the scene at the country club is rather evocative.*

You know, the critics questioned just that scene. They didn't get it, I guess. But it's not surprising. America then was feeling safe and sure of herself, a society primly sheltering its comfortable achievements and institutions. I don't remember *All That Heaven Allows*

Violence at the country club: Rock Hudson confronts the local business community and their wives in *All That Heaven Allows*

very well in detail, but I do recall the following influences on me. . . . One of the first of all American literary impacts on my thinking, when I was thirteen or fourteen, was a book my father gave me: *Walden* by Thoreau. This is ultimately what the film was about – but no one recognized it, except the head of the studio, Mr Muhl.

But you've even stuck the book into a close-up at the party. . . .

Yes, I had to; the producer suggested cutting it out, not quite knowing what it meant. But it stayed in. If I could remember, I could get together the oppositions in the film. But with a picture like that your only saving point is to take a tree out of the garden and put it down in a salon. It's antinomy again.

The picture is about the antithesis of Thoreau's qualified Rousseauism and established American society. It has a certain relationship, also, to *Take Me To Town*, which is about the American ideal of the simple, outdoor life. You know, when I first read *Walden* it was like a sun going up over my youth: this strangely *clean* language. And then in the wake of Thoreau I read Emerson, a bit

Hudson, Wyman and a tree (*All That Heaven Allows*)

later. I don't know how they'd look now, probably a bit dated, but then they had a strong effect on me. This kind of philosophy dwells in my mind and had to find an outlet eventually.

What is the Willa Cather novel which Rock Hudson gives to Dorothy Malone in The Tarnished Angels *– presumably this represents something of the same spirit, but referring to Nebraska rather than New England?*

That was *My Ántonia*: there's another influence. As I remember it, *My Ántonia* is a novel about circularity: the hero comes back to the place where he started out from. Today it would look passé, perhaps. But there was a time when I was deeply in love with America, a love that was shaken, though, to a degree, by wars and by Hiroshima, and by the things that happened afterwards, McCarthyism and so on. But sitting here in most orderly Switzerland, reliable as a good watch which is running to your expectations, I sometimes still would love to be back in the West. In Oregon, with its dark greens. In the desert, with its yellow light. Talking of Oregon, do you know H. L. Davis –

a writer I love? His *Honey in the Horn*? It's about the West, about a relatively recent West, perhaps truer than sometimes in the pictures. And there's a couple of other books he wrote which I love: *Team Bells Woke Me* and *Winds of Morning*. It's wonderful up in the North-West, sheltering woods, open country. Old farms. Oldness. . . . But let's get back to the pictures I made and leave the ones I would like to have done.

Well, there's Sign of the Pagan, *which was done before* All That Heaven Allows *and which needs discussing, because this seems a slightly bizarre component in your work: is it right that you were assigned to it rather late on, that someone else was supposed to do it?*

Yes, that is right.

A friend who saw it asked if you might ever have staged Marlowe's Tamburlaine?

I'll tell you about this picture. I was handed the script rather late by the studio. At that time we did have one star around, Jeff Chandler. He had read the script, but had refused to play the Attila part. Now the thing about Marlowe is precisely that I had suggested to Universal that I might shoot *Tamburlaine* instead – a play which I had never staged. But they wanted something less colossal, less frightening, and with religion in it – and there is no religion that would do for them in *Tamburlaine*.

I had been rather keen on doing the Marlowe, because he was someone who had exercised a very great effect on me early on in life. When I was about sixteen I saw a production of his *Dr Faustus*, which is a very impressive play, even if not as sweeping as Goethe's *Faust*. But I liked the baroque Renaissance quality of Marlowe's piece, the masks and symbols, and I admired him.

To do the Marlowe play as a picture, my taking-off point, as I remember it, would have been the following: at the start of the second act, in the saintly belief that an oath is not binding when it has been made to infidels, Sigismund of Hungary and the Christian lords of Bohemia and Buda break their pledge of peace and coexistence and treacherously attack the Turks. Now, I think this could have made an even more interesting religious angle than the one in *Sign of the Pagan*, which is simply the antithesis of the immovable church and the conquering lust of Attila.... Anyway, that had been my original idea about *Tamburlaine*, and I put it up as an alternative to *Sign of the Pagan*. It was turned down. Naturally. But I still think it might have gone well as a movie.

I had a very good writer on the picture with me, Barre Lyndon. He was schooled in Marlowe, Ben Jonson, Shakespeare. I was planning to do the Marlowe picture with him. I'm sure there is some very good dialogue by him in *Sign of the Pagan*.

So, anyway, I was stuck with the *Sign of the Pagan* script and a star who did not want to play the lead. Now, apart from Chandler the studio had one other person they were trying to promote, Ludmilla Tcherina, who had figured in *The Red Shoes*. All she could do was dance – though I got on well with her. She had a good body, but she could do nothing with her face. Any emotion she may have had must have gone straight down to her feet.

I needed someone to play the all-important Attila part, and the picture was in a hurry. Chandler's definite attitude was that he had to be the good guy, a screen lover, and that it would be bad for his career to play what he called the heavy. I think he liked the idea of himself striding around in a toga and all that. Whereas my position was that the only interesting thing in the story was the fury of Attila ... this man pacing around himself and his impossible goal, trying to capture the citadel of religion, Rome, circling it like an animal. Attila is one of these characters turning around themselves I like so much. He fits into my gallery – only he is a *violent* deviation from this usually quiet, Hamlet-like character. But this, more or less, was all there was that interested me. I honestly told Chandler this: that in my shooting of the picture the centre of attention would be Attila. He still wouldn't hear of it. 'Let them love me,' he said. And I wasn't unhappy. Chandler wouldn't have been able to bring out the twilighty aspect of the character.

Now, there was a lesser-known actor around, Jack Palance. He was famous, but not a leading man. The exhibitors didn't like him. I screened one of his pictures and I reckoned he might be all right in the part, if he had the strength to carry the picture. I pretty soon found out he did have sufficient presence on the screen. Everyone had told me he would be difficult to get along with. But I found him most pliable. Palance immediately liked the idea of doing Attila. He was

Sign of the Pagan: Jack Palance with Rita Gam (Kubra)

saying things like, 'Great, there I can grab an iron bar and smash in his skull.' I said to Chandler, 'Look out, because the part of the Hun is going to dominate the movie.' But he just said, 'I've never been upstaged by a heavy.' And, as you know, it came out Palance's film.

In a way, the same problem of balance which applied to the Attila and Chandler parts also went for the two female roles. The part of Kubra, Attila's daughter (Rita Gam), was much the more interesting part, for which I would have liked a less pretty girl, more ferociously handsome, and then to bend her over to the other side.

Did you choose the title?

Yes, I did, and it got me a very bad name as a title-chooser, although I liked it a lot. It is maybe one of the very few good things about the picture, which is one of my worst. There was a whole string of suggestions for titles, and it became a subject of dispute. Chandler hated the title because it obviously refers to the other guy, Attila, and he was always asking me to change it. But I'd like to come back to the question of titles later.

The only other thing I'd like to mention is that it was a costume picture, and costumes are very difficult for films. Films are too realistic. It is all right in something like the Vidocq picture (*A Scandal in Paris*) because that is a comedy, it's not realistic.

103

How did you find Cinemascope, which you used here for the first time?

The main thing was that with *Sign of the Pagan*, and the other Cinemascope pictures I did, I was required to shoot so that the film would fit both the new Cinemascope screen and the old-size screen. You had one camera, and one lens, but you had to stage it so that it would fit both screens. This is just as tough as doing a picture in two versions was in Germany. So I wasn't happy with the picture, and it was good to get away after that and go to my beloved Ireland.

How did you come to get so fond of Ireland?

Well, I had read a lot of Irish literature as a young man in Germany. And then when Mrs Sirk and I were going to America the boat anchored off Ireland. A wonderful odour of meadows came drifting across the sea, an odour of peace and farming life. You could really smell it, and visualize the playboy of the Western world roaming the wild beaches of Mayo.[4] And the contrast between the tranquillity of Ireland and all the lamenting people on the boat, which was the last boat out of Holland, was just amazing. That's when I realized that I would want to go back there – and I did, twice. First to pick the locations for *Captain Lightfoot*. And then to do the shooting. I had a great time. I went round to all those grand houses, and met all the owners to ask them if we could use their mansions in the picture. They were all delighted to earn a bit of money on the side.

I was surprised how much sunshine you got, considering it was Ireland.

We hardly got any. Most of it was shot in the rain. When we started shooting we were standing in one of those things you must know very well, having lived in Ireland – an Irish ruin. And we were waiting there in that special kind of Irish rain which is not really rain and Glassberg, my cameraman – whom I liked very much – said, 'You know, Douglas, here we just can't get anything.' I said to him, 'Irving, the word "can't" unfortunately doesn't exist in pictures. Let's put on this lens,' which I thought would best get the light and the depth of focus needed – because rain, of course, obscures distance.

The Irish revolution, the duel as comedy: Rock Hudson in *Captain Lightfoot*

So we shot a bit of stuff and sent the sample up to the lab in Dublin and it came back and it was good. So I said, 'Irving, let's go on.' We had a few booster lights and it came out handsomely, even though it was practically all shot in the drizzle. In Hollywood you have a light which is really too strong, too splendid. With Metty I always had a filter in front of my lens. This constant change of light in Ireland in a way matched the course of the story. The good are the bad, and the bad are the good. And the gambling, which goes far beyond my beloved but more rational chess, which could never have served the whirling and unpredictable cause of the revolution. I especially love the idea of a revolution financed from gambling – and the Irish were particularly enthusiastic whenever the English lost. And the other thing is that Hudson was playing comedy, and I realized his talents might lie there.

Even the duel is played rather like a comedy.

That's right. I think the duel must have been out of nostalgia for my old project, *Dreiklang*. In the Pushkin duel one man refuses to shoot. So I shoved in some comedy here. He smokes a cigar and

The American bourgeois family: Barbara Stanwyck visits the Groves, Fred MacMurray and Joan Bennett, in *There's Always Tomorrow*

shoots a scarecrow. I remember the Irish people who read the script were worried that their revolution should have comedy elements in it.

Anyway, I have a happy memory of this picture. We shot it one hundred per cent on location, like *The First Legion* and *Taza*.

Do you follow the events in Northern Ireland at all – because there is a weird combination of religion, violence, alcohol, and other elements you're interested in?

Indeed I do. I keep saying to Mrs Sirk that what's going on up there is the most interesting thing that's happened in the last ten years. It's real drama ... the Middle Ages. That guy Paisley is out of a play.

Do you want to say anything about There's Always Tomorrow?

I can't remember it, but I don't have an entirely bad feeling about it. MacMurray was a very good actor, and he was ambiguous in this: a successful man, but a failure in his own house. He has a toy factory, which he cannot break away from, like he can't break away from his past. He is like a naïve American boy who has never grown up. And then Stanwyck comes back from his past – but she doesn't find a grown man. She leaves. I think I became the victim of an unfinished thought from *Stopover* (*All I Desire*), which I tried to continue, but it didn't work out.

Both MacMurray and Stanwyck were excellent. But I think there was probably a flaw in the casting of the other woman, and in the writing. And the other thing was that the picture needed colour, which was planned.

The past coming back or catching up with one is a theme in many of your movies. In A Scandal in Paris, *I think Sanders actually says, 'Our past is catching up with us.'*

Yes, it is in several of my pictures. The circle ... and, of course, there is the parallel theme of regression which you will find, say, in *Written on the Wind*.

Yet, although the characters in Written on the Wind *do say, 'How far we have come from the river', children don't always seem to be having what you could call a good time in your movies. And they loom large in at least half a dozen of your films, often as conservatives, like in* All That Heaven Allows. *Can you tell me what your attitude towards them is?*

I like young children a lot. I had wonderful children in *Take Me To Town*; they were really great. I did *Weekend with Father* only for the children. And I loved the children on the Korean picture (*Battle Hymn*), maybe because of their foreignness.

I am extremely interested in the contrast between children and adults: there is a world looking at another world which is going downhill, but this new world does not yet know if its own fate will be the same. . . . The look of a child is always fascinating. It seems to be saying: is that what fate has in store for me, too?

The point is: are children really pure? I don't think so. The innocence they have will be destroyed. They are symbols of melancholy, not of purity. Children are usually put into pictures right at the end to show that a new generation is coming up. In my films I want to show exactly the opposite: I think it is the tragedies which are starting over again, always and always. . . .

Children and parents: the summer camp in *Weekend with Father* (Van Heflin on the left)

I once had a project for making a film about the Children's Crusade, an old Ufa project. Do you know about the Children's Crusade? Somewhere in Europe, during the period of the crusades, children wanted to serve God and imitate their fathers by going to the Holy Land, against the will of their parents. They all died. This is one of the great tragedies of history, or maybe just of legend. But Ufa turned it down because they were worried about there not being a full-grown star – and I planned to make it just a piece about children. No adults at all. And not just good children. Bad children also, especially the older ones, the domineering ones – because you can be sure that on an expedition of this kind you'd get a lot of the worst kids in Europe. And this is why it came to a bad end. You would have felt the bad elements blooming: this is what could have been such a pessimistic mirror of the adult world. I was so keen on the idea that after no one would make a picture out of it I told the story to a friend of mine, Eugene Vale, and he did a play on it.

The child is rather important in the way Never Say Goodbye *works out, too.*

'The look of a child is always fascinating. It seems to be saying: is that what fate has in store for me too?' Peter Bosse gazes down the staircase at his foster-mother (*Schlussakkord*)

Well, I'm not responsible for this picture.

What happened on it?

I brought over Cornell Borchers from Germany, and I did some work on preparing it. But then I had to leave it to do *Written on the Wind*, and later I was brought back to finish it as best I could. I think there was some good stuff by Jerry Hopper in it.

I'm extremely puzzled as to why you made Battle Hymn. *Who was this guy Dean Hess, who was killing people one day and saving kids the next? I read something about him in the* Reader's Digest *which seemed to sum up the contradiction, presumably unwittingly: 'War for Dean Hess was a complex business. He was in Korea on a dual mission: officially to eliminate as many of the enemy as he could; personally, to save as many Korean children as possible.'[5] What kind of a guy was he?*

An ambiguous character, in other words highly interesting as a subject for drama. Hess combined a soldier's attitude with a preacher's. He was sufficiently naïve to undertake that, and sufficiently bright to realize the contradiction within him.

How did you get into it in the first place?

It was a project of the front office, by Edward Muhl. I don't know whether I was at first interested or not, because it was a biography, by a living person, and I don't believe in making biographies. But I was interested in doing a flying picture. I have always been fascinated by flying, as you know. In the navy I flew in a plane searching the Baltic for mines, which were then shot from minesweepers. I wanted to get out to the Far East, to see Korea and especially Japan, which I had always wanted to visit, mainly to see the Japanese theatre: the Nō, the Kabuki, and the puppet plays, which I have been interested in since my early life. Especially in the theatrically enigmatic form of the Nō – part opera, part Zen Buddhism, part lyrical poem, and altogether product, and, by now, epitaph of a feudal hierarchy. I had a great time there. I met an Irish doctor who lived in Tokyo, who was also an excellent pianist, and he showed me round. And then Korean culture was perhaps even more interesting to me than Japanese culture, because it was a peasant culture and less known. By the way, I saw a most interesting production of *Richard III* there. It was all in Korean, so I couldn't understand the words, but it was a great and naïve production. They had transformed the character of Richard to make him very snake-like, which is a possible literal interpretation of the play.

But Dean Hess must have been a very strange guy?

Strange, yes. A flyer, and a preacher; a man trying to come to terms with having killed. There's a book by Ward L. Miner[6] on Faulkner, in which he quotes a passage from *Light in August*: 'Their escape is in violence, in drinking and fighting and praying.' *And in praying*: note the place of religion. The juxtaposition of violence and praying forms *Battle Hymn* also. The whole saving of children comes out of killing children. Because, you remember, he'd bombed that orphanage in Germany and felt guilty.

I had a lot of problems because he was on the set, hanging around, supervising every scene. I couldn't bring out the ambiguity of the

The Korean People's Army fighting off American aggression (*Battle Hymn*)

character as I would have liked. There was a magnificent chance here to make a film about killing and flying. This ties up with the Faulkner themes Miner talks about – 'aeroplane as the symbol of materialism'.

But you confuse the issue a bit by the way you have him leave the church and go off. There's the conversation with his wife after the sermon, and he says something like 'the sermons are going very badly, my heart isn't in this preaching, I'd better go to Korea.'

This isn't meant to mislead. It is *not* something supplementary; it is not extra to the character. He would have been like that. It's going in a circle. He is dancing his rondo – going back to the other thing he could do well: being a flyer. It is an almost cynical move, an escape – in the way Faulkner uses this word – an escape into patriotism, into fighting for his country. Dying maybe, as well as dishing out death. A confused decision – as confused a decision as people would make in such a mental condition. It is full of precise logic. But in Korea he never quite came back to complete the circle. He saw a chance to make good in flying, in bucking danger, but through the saving of children. He never flew another bombing mission after this had dawned on his goddam mind, and from then on he was preaching with his aeroplane, saving children. I've been talking about dancing a rondo – look at him going back to finish the circle now, at the beginning of which stands the destruction of a children's orphanage, and killing children, at the end there is saving children's lives and building an orphanage on the island of Cheju.

But this was all I could do because he was on the set. I had a problem with the transition, though. I had the idea that after he leaves the church he should drink, because it's a first ladder of escape which would prove not to take him to solid ground, and the house is afire. He is a man not able to find his identity, not until he has been killing. At any rate, putting in some structural element like him becoming a drunkard would have strengthened the character. And then we could have had him quit flying because of drink. At the moment, his quitting is only standing on one foot; drink would have given it two. But he was there on the set the whole time saying 'I didn't drink' and all that, trying to make me stick to 'truth'. He was as disturbing as the Jesuits on *First Legion*. I tried hard to convince him it would make a better movie, and that a guy like him *could* have taken to drink, but he wouldn't hear of it. So he remains this strange guy, which by God he is. But man is not created by reason, but by a different brand of logic, indecipherable to him.

I know you don't like *Battle Hymn*. I don't quite, either. But my reservations are of a very different sort. They are not directed towards the character of Dean Hess, but towards myself, or rather my handling of the casting. Because, you remember, I was talking about immovable characters and split ones and I told you Rock Hudson's talent made him cut out for an immovable role. But here I had to cast him – and unfortunately gave him the part of a split character. An actor like Stack would have been much more fitting, I'm sure. Just think of *Written on the Wind*, or *The Tarnished Angels*, a flyer's picture, too. Dean Hess properly cast would have belonged to the gallery of my vacillating characters. This I felt when I was trying to insert the drinking.

For two reasons I, the director, didn't succeed in bending Rock's talent to this type of broken personage. The first reason being his straight goodness of heart and uncomplicated directness. Before the camera you just can't cheat. The camera has X-ray eyes. It penetrates into your soul. You can't hide from the camera what you are – which I think is the great thing about cinematography, for on the stage you certainly can, with masks and make-up and I tell you the more make-up and masks you have, the more stylization, the better your play.

The other reason being the following: during the early part of the shooting, on location, I broke my leg. A rather complicated affair it was, and after a week's stay in hospital I had to finish the picture in a wheel-chair. To a degree this removes the director from his actors and his camera: you can't act out a scene, demonstrate it. It's tough to look through the lens and so you let certain things go you probably otherwise wouldn't. In addition to which, of course, Dean Hess's presence on the set became more felt in the picture and I don't have to tell you he was highly enthusiastic at being portrayed by that handsome straightforward giant, Rock Hudson.

But how do you feel about making a film about the Korean War, which was an imperialist war, without taking any critical distance on it? The film is actually introduced and presented by General Earle Partridge, who commanded the Fifth Air Force in the Korean War. So it does come across with a certain angle to it.

The Korean War was there. There was no reason as an afterthought to preach that the Korean War was bad, or good. It was almost history. The war as a fact was unalterable. There is nothing about taking sides, and *Battle Hymn* certainly doesn't concern itself with the fact of war but with a character in war. I know nothing about the prologue – I certainly didn't shoot it. And I've never been to the première of any of my pictures. Usually I don't see them after the last cut, because if you see them you think of tearing them apart and starting all over again.

Can we go on to Interlude, *which you made just after* Battle Hymn?

Of all the pictures I have done – except the Columbia pictures – *Interlude* is the one on which I had the least to do with the development of the story. My assistant and the cameraman, Bill Daniels, had already pre-researched locations for me, and since *Battle Hymn*, having a pretty complicated shooting schedule, had been delayed a bit, the studio was anxious to get on with *Interlude*. June Allyson had a finishing date in her contract and so I was forced to start as quickly as possible with the shooting. As a matter of fact, I wasn't even given a rest and had to fly to Bavaria with my leg still in a cast right after

I finished the cutting of *Battle Hymn*. So the story is in no way mine.

Again, it's supposed to be based on a Stahl film, When Tomorrow Comes, *and originally on a James Cain story – is that right?*

Yes, I think it is. As far as I know, I was given an outline based on the Stahl picture, which had originally been extremely loosely based on *Serenade* by Jimmy Cain. But the script I was given bore no resemblance to the Jimmy Cain story, with the exception of one sequence, the scene in the flooded church, which was anyway completely transposed for the picture. The Stahl film had already gone a long way from Jimmy Cain's story, and at the time I was making *Interlude*, I did not know that *Serenade* was anywhere behind it at all. I only found out afterwards that Universal had owned *Serenade* for years, and that the Stahl picture, too, had been based on it. If conditions had been different, and especially if I had had a different script based on the original James Cain novel, I think it could have been a terrific picture – at least a very unusual one.

The main fault with *Interlude* is that it didn't present characters which got me excited. And, in addition to my being handicapped by my leg, there was another problem: Brazzi was not exactly a born conductor. I had to spend more cutting time on the picture than on any other I ever made – you can still see it if you look carefully.

It's noticeable that both Written on the Wind *and* The Tarnished Angels, *which I think are your best films, were both produced by Zugsmith. How was this?*

Written on the Wind was an idea of Zug's. He was doing some lively work at the time, and we got on just great: for instance, he also produced Welles's *Touch of Evil*, which Orson was shooting on the next stage at Universal when I was doing *The Tarnished Angels*. And Zugsmith was the first person in Hollywood who was willing to take on the Faulkner book, *Pylon*, this old project and favourite of mine. Zug was also the only producer I could persuade to reject a happy end. *The Tarnished Angels* almost offers itself to have a happy end: Rock Hudson and Malone, now she's a widow, could go off together,

Interlude: even flowers cannot conceal Rossano Brazzi's dilemma, as the Countess (Françoise Rosay) calls him away from his wife (Marianne Cook) to see the visiting American with whom he has fallen in love

happily ending your picture. Instead of that, it's just a cool and friendly parting of ways; the observer remains there on his solid ground, and the girl moves away, again in a plane, if only a commercial one – there's the plane again, taking the girl out of the story.

Written on the Wind *is sometimes alleged to be a re-make of Fleming's* Reckless*: is that right?*

I never heard of *Reckless.* So far as I know, Zug owned the novel by Robert Wilder and we did a treatment on that. The writer was George Zuckerman, who had done *Taza* for me, and he did another good job. What the movie has is power and guts. I think it is my most gutty picture, which naturally is due to some extent to the material. Now, since you mention *Written on the Wind* and *The Tarnished Angels* together, I would like to point out a difference between these two pictures which otherwise have many things in common, like cast, producer, writer. *Written on the Wind* is much more typically American than the rather esoteric and introverted *The Tarnished Angels*, which deals with a very unordinary group of people who by

115

now have vanished from the American scene. But how does *Written on the Wind* look now? Nothing ages like pictures.

It has a great density of themes – money, alcohol, sex. It looks as if you had a cast you liked and good conditions: it has beautiful camerawork, lighting, and sets. I think it's a fine movie. It holds up very well – it hasn't dated. I think one of the Cahiers *reviewers said it was ten times more powerful than* Giant, *with which I'd agree, entirely.*

It was a piece of social criticism, of the rich and the spoiled and of the American family, really. And since the plot allowed for violence, it allowed for power of presentation also. Just observe the difference between *All That Heaven Allows* and *Written on the Wind*. It's a different stratum of society in *All That Heaven Allows*, still untouched by any lengthening shadows of doubt. Here, in *Written on the Wind*, a condition of life is being portrayed and, in many respects, anticipated, which is not unlike today's decaying and crumbling American society. Of course, as I was hinting at before, there is the contrast of the still intact represented by Mitch Wayne (Rock Hudson) and Lucy Hadley (Lauren Bacall). Now these two were, box-office-wise, the real stars of the picture. And I think this was then, as before, a happy combination – to put your star values not into the so-called interesting parts, but to strengthen the other side by good names and first-rate acting. For an actor an eccentric role like the Stack or Malone parts certainly is always more rewarding to play than the straight one. Now, this picture offered a quartet of equally competent performances and, as you know, Malone and Stack got Academy nominations. And there's another thing – and please don't smile at what I'm about to say – I had not only one split character in the picture, but two, performing their un-merry-go-rounds.

Written on the Wind, as I said, was quite different from my next Zugsmith picture, *The Tarnished Angels*. But, in a way, *The Tarnished Angels* grew out of *Written*. You had the same pair of characters seeking their identity in the follow-up picture; the same mood of desperation, drinking, and doubting the values of life, and at the same time almost hysterically trying to grasp them, grasping the wind. Both pictures are studies of failure. Of people who can't make a

Written on the Wind: Dorothy Malone drives the unreciprocating Rock Hudson through the Hadley oil-fields; and the servants look on as Malone faces her drunken brother Kyle (Robert Stack)

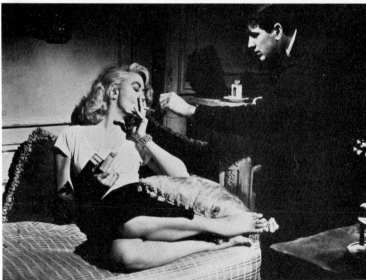

The Tarnished Angels: a party for the dead (above). Robert Middleton (Matt Ord) and Rock Hudson (Burke Devlin) drink with the flyers to the memory of Robert Stack (Roger Shumann); and (below) Hudson with Dorothy Malone (Laverne Shumann), clutching the first book she has read since she was sixteen – Willa Cather's *My Antonia*

success of their lives. Not the immensely rich ones, as in *Written on the Wind*, nor the down-at-heel bunch of flyers in *The Tarnished Angels*.

In the Cahiers *interview you spoke about your passionate interest in failure.*

Yes, but in French *échec* means much more than that: it means no exit, being blocked; and for this very reason it is a most valuable term. But *échec* in the sense both of failure and being blocked is indeed one of the few themes which interest me passionately. Success is not interesting to me. And the end of *Written on the Wind* is highly significant as far as this is concerned: Malone has lost everything. I have put up a sign there indicating this – Malone, alone, sitting there, hugging that goddamned oil well, having nothing. The oil well which is, I think, a rather frightening symbol of American society.

I'm not interested in failure in the sense given it by the neo-romantics who advocate the beauty of failure. It is rather the kind of failure which invades you without rhyme or reason – not the kind of failure you can find in a writer like Hofmannsthal. In both *Written on the Wind* and *The Tarnished Angels* it is an ugly kind of failure, a completely hopeless one. And this, again, is why the concept of *échec* is so good: there is no exit. All the Euripidean plays have this no exit – there is only one way out, the irony of the 'happy end'. Compare them with the American melodrama. There, in Athens, you feel an audience that is just as happy-go-lucky as the American audience, an audience that doesn't want to know that they could fail. There's always an exit. So you have to paste on a happy end. The other Greek tragedians have it, but with them it is combined with religion. In Euripides you see his cunning smile and his ironic twinkle.

That is where the flashback comes in. In *Written on the Wind*, as in *Summer Storm*, you start with an end situation. The spectator is supposed to know what is waiting for him. It is a different type of suspense, or anti-suspense. The audience is forced to turn its attention to the *how* instead of the *what* – to structure instead of plot, to variations of a theme, to deviations from it, instead of the theme itself. This is what I call the Euripidean manner. And at the end there is no solution of the antitheses, just the *deus ex machina*, which today is called the 'happy end'.

Going on to *The Tarnished Angels*, I told you that I had thought of trying to make a picture out of *Pylon* back in my Ufa days, but it was turned down. *Pylon* impressed me with its characters, and I was always very interested in flying, as you know.

Where did the title The Tarnished Angels *come from, because it's good?*

That was thought up by someone among the Universal salesmen. It is good. *Pylon* doesn't work as a title.

Faulkner had been around in Hollywood a lot: did you have him working on the movie at all?

I didn't have him work on the *Pylon* script, because I didn't want it. And he didn't want it either. Faulkner always maintained he never understood the movies. I had Zuckerman working with me again, and I seem to remember that he was instrumental in selling it to Zugsmith: I think he interested Zugsmith in the Malone part, particularly the parachute jump. He (Zuckerman) understood that the story had to be completely un-Faulknerized, and it was.

Although the book is completely transformed I think the characters in the film are still pretty close to Faulkner's. This man (Stack) seeking his identity, a man standing on very uncertain ground. The ground doesn't give him any security, he is reaching for a certainty in the air – a crazy idea, and a grand one, I think. At the same time it's a love story – one of those off-love stories I have always wanted to make, which started with *Dreiklang*.

Now, to go back to casting. The character I was most interested in was the flyer, and I thought Stack was the right guy for that. As for Burke Devlin (Rock Hudson), in the novel the newspaperman is maybe too close to the world of the flyers. I thought it would be better to have a contrast, and I think in this way he becomes better integrated than he was in Faulkner's book. He is a neatly polished looking-glass held up to the crazy world of the flyers, these Indians of the air. He is the hub of the goings-on in both book and film. And I like the way he is not completely immovable. He changes. At first he is wide-eyed, rather innocent, just reflecting events – a mirror for the excentric and seemingly inhuman people and the immoral imagery of the action. Initially he does not take to the Shumann group, the flyers. But then his consciousness grows, it widens from a lame curiosity to fascination, which is sexual as well as just existing in his well-combed, well-ordered mind, shaped by a bourgeois world. And eventually he recognizes the gypsies of the air as having more solid ground under their feet than his own solid shoes are treading.

Of course, part of the change I had to make in the reporter's character was necessitated by Hudson's personality – if only because Hudson could not hope to match the physical characteristics Faulkner gave the reporter.[7]

By the way, you know that Faulkner was much influenced by Eliot, that great American-English poet, who was a huge influence on my and Faulkner's generation. The Eliot impact you can see best in *Pylon*. There is even a chapter called 'Lovesong of J. A. Prufrock', after one of the early great poems of Eliot. There are some lines in the Eliot poem I would like to read to you because on the set I read them to Hudson in order to give him an idea of what Faulkner had in mind with the reporter's character:

> 'No! I am not Prince Hamlet, nor was meant to be;
> Am an attendant lord, one that will do
> To swell a progress, start a scene or two,
> Advise the prince; no doubt, an easy tool,
> Deferential, glad to be of use,
> Politic, cautious, and meticulous;
> Full of high sentence, but a bit obtuse;
> At times, indeed, almost ridiculous –
> Almost, at times, the Fool.'[8]

This is what I wanted Hudson to be, and I told him so: 'You are not the prince in this movie,' I told him – 'that's Stack.' To my surprise, he understood, although he knew that this meant in a way he would have to play second fiddle. And, if anything, I accentuated the trend. 'Look,' I said, 'he watches these flyers, at first very much from the outside. But he also makes contact – you remember the scene with Malone: "deferential, glad to be of use".'

There is another Eliot theme in the story – and that is death by water. Stack knows the kid isn't his – and he decides to sacrifice himself, because that's the only worthwhile thing he can do. He's been escaping every day up into the sky in his plane, and now he

121

realizes he can do something. Do you remember the fourth section of *The Waste Land*? Let me read that to you as well, because I read this to Stack when we were shooting:

> 'Phlebas the Phoenician, a fortnight dead,
> Forgot the cry of gulls, and the deep sea swell
> And the profit and loss.
>   A current under sea
> Picked his bones in whispers. As he rose and fell
> He passed the stages of his age and youth
> Entering the whirlpool.
>   Gentile or Jew
> O you who turn the wheel and look to windward,
> Consider Phlebas, who was once handsome and tall as you.'[9]

Faulkner also talks about death by water. And those last lines are wonderful – that is Stack.

Again, I think this was a good film about an America of the past, and it got the mood of the Depression as well. You know, there are many aspects of American history you could make wonderful pictures about. Like the age of Jackson. No one makes pictures about the age of Jackson, but I think it's one of the turning points of American history, and there you could make a film just as good as any Lincoln picture.

But there is one other thing I want to mention about *The Tarnished Angels*: the irony of heroism. Miner's book on Faulkner I mentioned has some very interesting things in it. One of the things he discusses is just that kind of heroism. And he also has some very good stuff on the aeroplane, the plane as a symbol of materialism. Let me read you this: 'They have nothing but their plane ... part of civilization which has rooted them out of their soils. . . . Their escape is in violence, in drinking, in fighting and in praying.' I think this sums up very well the world of *Pylon*. And these Faulknerian elements are also very characteristic of Dean Hess, as I said before. There is a passage in *Pylon* which gets these flyers very well: 'They ain't human you see. No ties; no place where you were born and have to go back to it now and then even if it's just only to hate the damn' place good and comfortable for a day or two.'[10] The flyers in *Pylon* weren't human.

One of the people Miner mentions in the book about Faulkner,

Malone bids farewell to Stack as he takes off for the last time (above); and the Depression in New Orleans: death-masks, dancing, parties and a grand piano (*The Tarnished Angels*)

Royce, has something very good on this; he calls it *loyalty to a lost cause more than to a winning one.* That flying business was no good. They were only just scraping along, in fact they were losing. And then finally Stack finds a cause – to sacrifice himself. This is what Royce means: more people are committed to losing causes, often passionately committed, than is usually acknowledged.

How come you didn't get colour for this film?

They didn't trust the story. Then the picture was rather successful, and Zug wanted to do *The Unvanquished* with me, but it didn't work out. Zug left the studio, and I had to do *A Time to Love and a Time to Die.*

For which you went back to Germany.

Yes. Now this is a picture I want to say a few things about, because it raises rather a lot of issues. I think this is one of the pictures where I nearly succeeded in building a certain kind of film – an off-beat love story, the same thing I would have liked to do with *Shockproof* and perhaps more or less succeeded in doing with *The Tarnished Angels.* But first let me say something about the title. The title in a picture is like the prologue in a drama. Shakespeare was a great titles man, and I mind about them a lot. Titles are like signs in front of movies, or they should be: a passing in-between thing, not the drama itself. *Interlude*, for example, is a title which puts up a sign. It almost tells the story before you start, which I like. This is one of my principles – like what I was saying about the flashback. It *should* tell the story, but in a certain way; not the whole story. That's why *Stopover* would have been such a good title to have kept for *All I Desire*, which is very flat. *Stopover* would have been not just a sign, but an ironic sign.

Or take *All That Heaven Allows*: I just put this title there like a cup of tea, following Brecht's recipe. *There's Always Tomorrow* is another fair title. An ironic one, too. Tomorrow is the yesterday, and MacMurray will still be playing with his toys (the only reservation I had about that was that there have been too many 'tomorrow' titles). And *Imitation of Life* is more than just a good title, it is a wonderful title: I would have made the picture just for the title, because it is all there – the mirror, and the imitation, what I was saying about Strindberg.

There are one or two more: *Written on the Wind* – I like this title, too, because it is like *Interlude*: it conveys the feeling of frustration, which is certainly one of the themes of the picture, and I think the flashback works extremely well here together with the title, revealing something of the picture and thereby creating suspense. *Summer Storm* and *Battle Hymn* are not bad either, especially the latter: it's full of duplicity – the relationship between war and Christianity; there's the church, and right outside the church the battle and the killing are going on. The studio first suggested *Battle Song*, I believe, which is certainly one of the themes of the picture, and I think the 'battle' that really counts. *Sign of the Pagan* is a great combination. I got this title through by telling the studio about the success of *Sign of the Cross*, which is a lousy title as it happens, but anyway, the parallel convinced them – although the combination of 'sign' and 'pagan' is utterly removed from the combination of 'sign' and 'cross'. *Sign of the Cross*, you know what it is. *Sign of the Pagan*, you have to think: what is that? It gives you a lead, but without explaining everything to you.

Magnificent Obsession *is a striking title, as well.*

Yes, it is; there's some chemistry there, definitely. *A Time to Love and a Time to Die* is good because of the juxtaposition of 'love' and 'die'. What was interesting for me was the love affair between the soldier and the girl. I first wanted it to be called *The Lovers*, Fuller's old title for *Shockproof*, which Columbia rejected. They thought that 'love' wasn't good in a title. And in Hollywood this was almost a rule, not to have the word 'love' in front of a picture. Apparently this stemmed from a couple of pictures which, carrying a 'love' title, had been flops. Most picture-makers, as far as I know, obeyed the rule. Of course, there were exceptions, and I wasn't scared in insisting on having a 'love' title; and since *The Lovers* was turned down I went back to the title of Remarque's book, *A Time to Live and a Time to Die*, as it was in German – a title we slightly changed for the non-German distribution into *A Time to Love and a Time to Die*. I was so insistent on this, for I felt it had to be a love story, mainly. The denunciation of Nazidom would have to take second place to the love story. You see, this picture was made in 1957. Hitler's empire of a thousand years was history. Furthermore, I thought 'die' balanced 'love' very well. And going back to my idea of a title being a kind of prologue, it announces the theme of the picture. The terrible incongruity of killing and young love. I was enchanted to see that in *Cahiers* Godard did get the point, and made the title almost the base for his excellent and unusual review.[11]

Was the Remarque book difficult to adapt?

No, not at all. In a way it's written rather like a film script. Some critics blamed me for not portraying the Hitler period more 'critically'. What was interesting to me was a landscape of ruins and the two lovers. But again, a strange kind of love story, a love conditioned. Two people are not allowed to have their love. The murderous breath of circumstances prevents them. They are hounded from ruin to ruin. The lovers have nowhere to go for their love. Do you remember the scene in the old restaurant? The lovers are imitating the joyful life of a lost past. There is a moment of happiness. Seemingly. There is food. There are friendly lamps. There is light. Their love has restored the world. Bang! It is destroyed. I was striving for this relationship between their love and the ruins. I hope it came off: the portrayal of this young and desperate love. Not just a boy and girl story, but two lovers *in extreme circumstances.* . . . How does the picture look today?

It looks great.

I'm really glad, because I put a lot of myself into the love part of the picture. It is a story very close to my concerns, especially the brevity of happiness. I am not as pessimistic as I may sometimes appear. I do believe in happiness ... happiness must be there, because it can be destroyed. Besides, a flawless happiness would be like a badly written poem ... I think if a 'happy end' had been put on to *A Time to Love and a Time to Die* – which was logically possible within the framework of the story – you would not have had this impression of painful tenderness shared by the two lovers in their rare moments of happiness. Only things which are doomed can be so painfully tender. Things which last may have a certain beauty in themselves, but they do not have this strange power which only appears at certain moments like, for example, in the scene where Gavin and Pulver realize it is their duty to be happy since the world around them is collapsing: at this moment they have to enjoy their happiness to the maximum, they must get intoxicated on it. . . . True happiness never lasts.

I hope the desperation comes across. And the war part. Because there is some good war stuff there, I feel, not the usual phoney Hollywood stuff. And you never see the enemy, which I like.

How did it go down in Germany?

Badly, of course. They couldn't allow a refugee to give any kind of an interpretation of what life was like in Germany during the war. In Germany then, in the late fifties, everyone was full of self-pity. And today people still are, at least the generation of the war. I meet someone I knew from way back and he keeps telling me how bad things were for them, how they suffered, how they endured, how many examples he could give me of courage, and so on, and how splendid, comfortable, and serene the life of an émigré must have been. This is one of the reasons I couldn't live there any more.

Of course, the picture is not only a story of love. It is also, as in Remarque's book, a piece of social criticism, a political film. Not perhaps a nice one for Germans to look at. But there's a strange thing: in Russia it went on in one of the provinces and, as far as I know, was a big success. I was supposed to go over there, and then suddenly the invitation was withdrawn, along with the picture. I guess someone had noticed that at the end the Russian partisans shoot Gavin, the good German, and decided this was anti-Soviet. I was surprised, because it is a good, ironic ending, in the sense I've explained. It is anti-war, it is against killing, and it is anti-Nazi. What happened depressed me.

But I was even more depressed when the picture was banned in Israel, which only goes to show how close the opposites often are. Remarque said to me afterwards: 'How can you make a political film in these circumstances?' This ban in Israel was completely silly of course, and I never could find out the reason for it; censors apparently don't like to give reasons. Someone sent me a clipping from one of the Israeli newspapers where there was a heated protest against the censor for banning this profoundly anti-Nazi film. I personally think I should have cut out some of the more explicitly anti-Nazi material in order to be even more anti-Nazi, because less is very often stronger than more. But I didn't have a free hand.

You mean you'd have cut out things like the bonfire on the grand piano?

Yes, I would have liked to toss that out. This comes back to what I've said about social criticism: you must not be too explicit – and in a film about the Nazis you need perhaps be less explicit.

Is it right that Paul Newman was supposed to do the part originally?

Yes, I think he was, but then Universal wanted me to build a new star, who was Gavin. Anyway, I'm not sure that Newman would have been right for the part. Gavin, naturally, was not nearly the actor Newman was, he was more or less a complete beginner, even more so, I think, than Hudson was when I got him originally. But for this picture I felt, after extensive tests, that he could be just right because of his lack of experience. He was fresh, young, good-looking, not pretty though, earnest – and this little dilettante quality I figured would be quite the thing for the lead of this picture. A picture which had to be shot in almost documentary fashion, avoiding all so-called brilliance in acting. It shouldn't be the vehicle of a star. And this was the reason for picking Lilo Pulver, a young German actress, for the other part. She, too, was unknown in the States, though she had a small and good reputation in Europe. The two, I believe – and the Godard review in *Cahiers* encourages me to think so – were good, and simple (which are almost synonyms).

Can I come back to the cutting? You say you didn't have a free hand, yet the cutting seems to show your touch.

I finished the entire first rough cut of the picture in Germany before it went to Hollywood. Of course, I couldn't simply throw out sequences I had shot. But the whole architecture of the cut of the picture is mine.[12]

I think this picture illustrates quite well a thing I maybe learned from Dreyer – slow cutting, holding a shot that much longer than the average director does. I consider his late picture *Gertrud* a very great and subtle study. *Day of Wrath* I saw three or four times, and I thought it was fantastic. Before that, I was deeply impressed by *The Passion of Joan of Arc*. I learnt from it the importance of certain hesitating cuts, which throw tremendous emphasis on a story. Dreyer had developed this slowness to an almost unbearable degree, but there is the whole Middle Ages in it – its slow, precise, and deadly way of thinking. It harbours a threat by being so slow. You can see it in some of my pictures.

Like Imitation of Life?

To some extent.

How was Imitation of Life *put up to you, and did you see the old Stahl picture here?*

As far as I remember, Ross Hunter gave me the book, which I didn't read. After a few pages I had the feeling this kind of American novel would definitely disillusion me. The style, the words, the narrative attitude would be in the way of my getting enthusiastic. But Ross also had an outline done which closely followed the Stahl picture. The picture itself I didn't look at either, not at that time, at any rate. Later on I saw it, after I had finished my own picture. So I was free of any possible influence. I liked it, I thought it was very good, but it belonged to the previous generation. After I had read the outline, I made one change, socially – an important one, I think. In Stahl's treatment of the story the white and the Negro women are co-owners of a thriving pancake business – which took all the social significance out of the Negro mother's situation. Maybe it would have been all right for Stahl's time, but nowadays a Negro woman who got rich *could* buy a house, and wouldn't be dependent to such a degree on the white woman, a fact which makes the Negro woman's daughter less understandable. So I had to change the axis of the film and make the Negro woman just the typical Negro, a servant, without much she could call her own but the friendship, love, and charity of a white mistress. This whole uncertain and kind of oppressive situation accounts much more for the daughter's attitude.

129

The only interesting thing is the Negro angle: the Negro girl trying to escape her condition, sacrificing to her status in society her bonds of friendship, family, etc., and rather trying to vanish into the imitation world of vaudeville. The imitation of life is not the real life. Lana Turner's life is a very cheap imitation. The girl (Susan Kohner) is choosing the imitation of life instead of being a Negro. The picture is a piece of social criticism – of both white and black. You can't escape what you are. Now the Negroes are waking up to black is beautiful. *Imitation of Life* is a picture about the situation of the blacks before the time of the slogan 'Black is Beautiful'.

I tried to make it into a picture of social consciousness – not only of a white social consciousness, but of a Negro one, too. Both white and black are leading imitated lives. . . . There is a wonderful expression: seeing through a glass darkly. Everything, even life, is inevitably removed from you. You can't reach, or touch, the real. You just see reflections. If you try to grasp happiness itself your fingers only meet glass. It's hopeless.

But Imitation *is somehow like* Magnificent Obsession: *they both come from the same zone of what would be called 'the weepies', and have the sentimentality that goes with them.*

Exactly. And more or less I had the same tough time fighting this quality in *Imitation of Life* as in *Magnificent Obsession*, knowing also it couldn't be removed from the plot without the whole thing collapsing: that makes it so different from *The Tarnished Angels* or *Written on the Wind*. So you might count all four of them as melodramas.

Now here in *Imitation of Life*, as in the others, I had the contrast of interesting parts and star roles. Lana Turner and Gavin are taking more or less the positions of Bacall and Hudson in *Written on the Wind* or Hudson in *The Tarnished Angels*, while the Malone and Stack characters find their equivalent in the part of Susan Kohner (Sarah Jane Johnson). Again, the same phenomenon occurs – the supporting part is the more interesting and the better acting part. The better part for the director, too; he can make more out of it. Susan Kohner, a complete beginner in pictures, steps forward, putting Turner and Gavin into the shade.

There is another way in which I feel *Imitation of Life* and *Written*

'You don't believe the happy end, and you're not really supposed to'. Susan Kohner and Lana Turner (above), and Juanita Moore's funeral; both from the end of *Imitation of Life*

on the Wind, though so different, have something in common: it's the underlying element of hopelessness. In *Written on the Wind* the use of the flashback allows me to state the hopelessness right at the start, although the audience doesn't know the end. But it sets the mood. In *Imitation of Life*, you don't believe the happy end, and you're not really supposed to. What remains in your memory is the funeral. The pomp of the dead, anyway the funeral. You sense it's hopeless, even though in a very bare and brief little scene afterwards the happy turn is being indicated. Everything seems to be OK, but you well know it isn't. By just drawing out the characters you certainly could get a story – along the lines of hopelessness, of course. You could just go on. Lana will forget about her daughter again, and go back to the theatre and continue as the kind of actress she has been before. Gavin will go off with some other woman. Susan Kohner will go back to the escape world of vaudeville. Sandra Dee will marry a decent guy. The circle will be closed. But the point is you don't have to do this. And if you did, you would get a picture that the studio would have abhorred.

And this is where Euripides comes to the rescue again. Of course, I know this is a case of calling in the gods to witness in a dwarfish cause. Forgive me for unloading my classical education on you: do you know the last chorus of the *Alcestis*?

> 'The manifestations of Gods happen in many shapes
> Bring many matters to happy ends
> What we thought would happen does not happen
> The impossible is not impossible for the Unknowns
> And that is the way it has happened here and today.'

You see, there is no real solution of the predicament the people in the play are in, just the *deus ex machina*, which is now called 'the happy end', and which both Hollywood and Athenians and assorted Greeks were also so keen on. But this is what is being called Euripidean irony. It makes the crowd happy. To the few it makes the aporia more transparent. The theme is basic – I used it in *Magnificent Obsession*, which is in some ways rather like it.

To go back, though, to *Imitation of Life*: I think this picture also shows up one of the big differences between the media of the novel and the movies. The novel has never been subjected to something like Hollywood, to the pressure of time and big money, to sales people, producers, exhibitors – or at least not to such a degree – saying you've got to have a happy end even in the most goddam awful situations. With a novel you are more independent – at least as long as you are working. Until you have finished you are only answerable to your own artistic conscience.

When you made Imitation of Life *did you know you were leaving Hollywood? The funeral looks like a farewell, and the trajectory of the film, too, given the cast of actors, agents, producers, and so on, makes it look like this.*

In my mind I guess I was leaving Hollywood, yes, even before I made the picture. I had had enough. I most likely would have left even if illness hadn't coincided. Even though after *Imitation of Life* I might have been able to write my own ticket, because this was a very big success, certainly the biggest one Universal had ever had – its biggest money-maker of all time.

An indication of this might have been my insisting on the tearing up of the contract I had with Universal, which still had years to run. This was not unlike my leaving Leipzig, when Dr Goerdeler tried to stop me – though the general situation was very different. Universal tried to hold me too. And to me it was not happy leaving, in a way, because as I told you when talking about my Universal period, they were extremely decent to me. They had become my friends. My agent, like everyone else, considered my move a silly one. They told me, 'You're just reaching the peak of your career and you quit.' It certainly hadn't happened in Hollywood before, where success means everything. So no one understood.

I took a picture with a smaller company, a subject which interested me and which I was supposed to do entirely in France: the life of Utrillo, the painter – or rather of him and his mother, Suzanne Valadon, also a very good painter. I flew to Paris and tried to influence Ionesco to write the script. He consented, and he had interesting and unusual ideas; it would have been a good picture, which would have made it difficult for me to give up the movies entirely. But I fell ill. The doctor told me I would have to take at least a year off, if not more, and this became the definitive break with Hollywood and with picture-making. Later on, having become well again after a couple of years and probably able to go back to

Love among the ruins of Berlin: Lilo Pulver and John Gavin (a studio shot) in *A Time to Love and a Time to Die*

Hollywood, I had quite a number of offers: among others, *Madame X* – which is a glaring example. I really toyed with the idea of doing this picture. 'Bending' it again like I had done so often before to something which wasn't quite impossible, because the story – God knows – is. But then I realized all this was a thing of the past. I had outgrown this kind of picture-making which in a way was typical of Hollywood in the fifties and of American society, too, which then tolerated only the play that pleases, not the thing that disturbs the mind. I felt a totally new Hollywood would soon be in the making, a Hollywood open to pictures like *Easy Rider* – at any rate, pictures of a very different brand, and a different style. But I felt I wasn't young enough any more to wait this out, for just going on making pictures would have been ridiculous for me, because I had so many other interests that now had first place in my mind. Though, sometimes I pondered being back there again in Hollywood, experimenting, developing a completely new style, appropriate to a new time which I felt was coming. There is the undeniable lure of this rotten place, Hollywood, the joy of being again on the set, holding the reins of a picture, fighting circumstances and impossible stories, this strange lure of dreams dreamt up by cameras and men. And, in addition to that, as in my Roman days there was the lure of going back and completing a promising career. But I felt I had to stick to my decision to take my illness as more than coincidence. I honestly can't say I was entirely happy about this. I had no roots any more in Europe, and I don't think I wanted to sink new roots into ground that had become foreign to me. In the meanwhile I had become much more at home in America. But I knew that if I went back there I certainly wouldn't be able to resist being drawn into pictures again, so I stayed in Switzerland, where I am not at home either, and sometimes, thinking about myself, it seems to me I am looking at one of those goddam split characters out of my pictures.

NOTES

1. For Lang on this, see Peter Bogdanovich, *Fritz Lang in America*, London, 1967, pp. 76–7. For Losey on it, see *Losey on Losey*, ed. Tom Milne, London and New York, 1967, pp. 83–90.
2. Directed by Milestone (1947), from a novel by Remarque; the music was by Hanns Eisler, and the script is reputed to have been written or 'revised' by Brecht.
3. Joseph Pevney, 1951.
4. Synge's *The Well of the Saints* is a play whose thematic would seem rather close to that of Sirk. Based on an old French play, *Moralité de l'Aveugle et du Boiteux*, Synge's play has made the cripple blind as well. A miracle which heals both the men ruins their life of illusion, and they beg the saint to restore them to their previous condition of blindness.
5. Quentin Reynolds, 'The Battle Hymn of Dean Hess', *Reader's Digest*, March 1957, p. 84.
6. Ward L. Miner, *The World of William Faulkner*, Durham, N.C., 1952, p. 143 (*Light in August*, p. 347).
7. In Faulkner's book the reporter is rake-like, very tall and thin.
8. T. S. Eliot, *Collected Poems 1909–1962*, London, 1968, p. 17.
9. *Ibid.*, p. 75.
10. William Faulkner, *Pylon*, Signet Paperback Edition, New York, 1958, p. 30.
11. Jean-Luc Godard, 'Des Larmes et de la Vitesse', *Cahiers du Cinéma* 94 (April 1959). English translation in *Screen*, Vol. 12, No. 2 (Summer 1971).
12. As far as I can ascertain, Sirk shot the film to include certain scenes he personally did not want to have included. He then cut the film himself, including those scenes which he would have preferred to remove entirely. Both the shooting and the cutting were done by him, but the final form of the film was not exactly as he wished.

6: After Hollywood

But this wasn't the end of your career in show-business, was it? You did theatre work, as well as having offers from Hollywood, didn't you?

Yes, I did. Zug offered me *Confessions of an Opium Eater* (*Evils of Chinatown* or *Souls for Sale*) and another,[1] neither of which I did – I must confess, to my chagrin, because I like Zugsmith. His way of thinking, though certainly very different from mine, was original and very complementary to my own approach to pictures, which is always helpful.

I thought Confessions of an Opium Eater *came out an excellent movie. . . . Now we've talked about your films, could you say a little bit more about the directors you liked, and who influenced your work?*

Well, Dreyer and Renoir I've talked about already. Murnau certainly was a great influence and hit me earlier in life than Renoir – *Tabu* and *Sunrise* are both exceptional pictures; *Faust* less so, but probably you can't press Goethe's work into a picture – it is too big, too wide, the words are too important. The second part of the tragedy, especially, with its senile majesty, is out of the reach of picture-making, I think. Of Marlowe's work you could perhaps make a movie, and even a very modern one, with a very new technique.

A great movie-maker who influenced me early on was Lubitsch. He had a definite influence on certain sections of my theatre work, on my staging of comedies. He then was incredibly modern as a picture director – particularly one film, *The Marriage Circle* (1924), was very important to me in this respect. It had a kind of lasting impact. I value comedy greatly, as I've told you. Lubitsch was able to walk the *very* narrow path between the absurd and the realistic. And this ties up with another point: he also had taste and elegance, which I hope I learnt a little of from him. They certainly are essentials of picture-making.

To Be or Not To Be seems to me about the most extraordinary example ever of walking the narrow path, given its date (1942).

Exactly.

Did you ever see any of Ophüls's stage work in Germany, and was it at all like his movies, which I like a lot?

There were definite signs of a movie-maker's talents in his stage work: this is certainly true. Ophüls was somehow like Sternberg: he had a great gift for the impressionistic touch. I know from conversations with him that he regarded Sternberg as a decisive experience, which Sternberg also was for me, although in certain of his creations the splintering of images goes too far.

A very strange thing to me was a kind of difference between Ophüls's French movies (some of which, by the way, he did with Nebenzal, I believe) and his later American and, even more so, final European work. He was steadily growing in stature, I think, and developed fully only in America. Now, I don't mean to say his earlier pictures were weak, but there's a different handwriting compared to the later ones, and I do think the American period, though not especially rewarding to him, helped him to arrive at his most personal style. Now, I think it shows best in *Letter from an Unknown Woman*, though it is not as perfect as *Madame de . . .* , which I value very highly.

And Ford?

I love him.

I'm glad you do, but in some ways he seems a slightly bizarre preference.

Bizarre? Not at all, at least it now seems to me as natural as my general interest in and liking of things American. I've loved Ford from way, way back – this is long before I went to the States – and I remain an ardent admirer of his works: pictures like *How Green Was My Valley*, or *The Searchers*, or *The Man Who Shot Liberty Valance* are wonderful, full of cinematic wonders. And then I came to like the unmistakable Irish element in him, a good combination with Western flair. In America I discovered that he was famous more for films like *The Grapes of Wrath* which to me aren't nearly so impressive as some of his Western work.

But you know I love the Western. Now, there weren't too many Hollywood directors then who would have agreed, and even less critics. I remember when Ford made his famous pronouncement: 'My name's John Ford. I make Westerns,' this caused perplexity in Hollywood. It was the first time people there started to think about the Western as a medium worthy of great attention, except as a solid, ever-saleable piece of merchandise. There was no understanding of the place of the Western in the American cinema, or of the place of pictures in American culture. Ford's remark set off a big discussion: people were so surprised that the great John Ford had chosen to categorize himself like that. They couldn't understand it. They would have rather expected him to step forward as the creator of *The Grapes of Wrath*. But any appreciation of the American cinema, I think, involves an appreciation of the Western and also of the melodrama, and you can achieve this via a specifically *cinema* criticism. As someone who started out as a theatre man, and a director of mostly highly literary plays I'd like to go emphatically on the record with that.

Were you at the meeting where De Mille was attacking Mankiewicz and Ford made that remark? What was it like?

I was at the meeting, yes. Well, as you know, almost everybody in Hollywood was rather reactionary. Ford, like most of the others, was very conservative indeed. But he wasn't as bad as De Mille. De Mille was a petrified old man. And I think his pictures are petrified. Ford was a very fair guy, though, as well as being conservative.

Which of the young American directors did you like?

The one I liked very much on the Universal lot was Budd Boetticher. He was often on the next lot to me, and we'd meet in the morning on the way to work, and I'd say to him, 'Hi there, Budd, what are you doing?' And he'd say, 'Hi there, Doug, oh just some lousy old Western – how about you?' And I'd say, 'Oh, just some lousy old melodrama,' and we'd go on our way. But I thought he had a completely new, fresh, modern approach to Westerns, by which I don't mean the psychoanalytic approach – things like *High Noon* and *Hud* – which was nonsense. I like Boetticher's work a lot. One other person there I can remember I was very much interested in was Blake Edwards, whom I first met as a writer before he developed into an excellent and original creator of comedy.

You did, though, go back to Germany once in a while after you left Hollywood. I'm very interested in the whole question of the changes wreaked on Germany culturally by Nazism; when you went back after the war, did you find the cultural situation much changed – and was it possible to re-integrate yourself into it in any way?

Well, it was changed in many ways. But I should first say one thing about this, which we touched on earlier: that a great part of the German intelligentsia, the vast majority of the non-Jewish one, went along with Hitler, or became downright Nazis. And my main feeling when I went back after the war was that the place was unreconstructed. And still is, in a way. There has not been any profound break with Nazism nor, most important, with the earlier elements in German culture which had contributed to Nazism (which is why so many leading cultural figures could deceive themselves into siding with the Nazis). I found West Germany an extremely hypocritical and strangely materialistic society.

Now, after my unhappy experience when I first went back in 1949–50, I did go back again in the early 60s, to do some theatrical work. I still had a reputation from before I left, and so it was possible for me to go back and stage some plays, which filled up my time. With the other movie directors who had gone to Hollywood it was rather different; I think only Siodmak and Lang were exceptions. While the German theatre survived, the German cinema was wrecked: by the Nazis in the first place, then with a supplementary blow when the Americans dissolved Ufa. You could say, very roughly, that the Nazis destroyed the tradition of German cinema,

Later theatre work: Sirk's production of Schiller's *The Parasite* (Munich, 1966), with Kurt Meisel, centre left, in the lead

German painting, German literature. Whereas theatre, music – and particularly the performance of music – had survived, although in a very conservative way. So it was altogether a changed country I found: not only the hypocrisy I encountered there upset me, but fire and life had gone out of thinking. Germans are unaware of the dominant undercurrent. They see what is on the surface and are happy to imitate that. Everything there is still an imitation. And someone like Lang, I think, had apparently to go right back to the past when he returned: he was unable to find any new elements in postwar Germany for his pictures.

What theatre work have you done in Germany in recent years?

I've just staged a few plays, mostly at the Residenztheater in Munich: I put on there *Cyrano de Bergerac*, *Le Roi Se Meurt* by Ionesco, *The Tempest*, Schiller's *The Parasite*, and Molière's *The Miser*. I had Kurt Meisel in the lead in three of these: in *Cyrano*, in *The Parasite*, and in the Ionesco. He had been in several of my pictures in the 1930s, and now has become the head of the Residenztheater. And then last year (1969) I put on Tennessee Williams's last play, *The Seven Descents of Myrtle*, in Hamburg. But now I feel no urge to go back there at all.

And I think that's it. A long day's journey. . . . The end of a circle. Now, don't take this as resignation. There's still a lot that heaven allows.

NOTE

1.   *Fanny Hill*, then made by Zugsmith himself (1964).

140

Biofilmography

Douglas Sirk was born in Hamburg on 26 April, 1900, of Danish parents. His early childhood was spent in Skagen, on the north tip of Jutland, in Denmark. After that he lived in Hamburg. Sirk's original name was Hans Detlef Sierck; his theatre work up to 1926–27 was under this name; from then onwards all his work in Germany in both theatre and cinema was as Detlef Sierck. On arrival in the US, he altered his name to Douglas Sirk. His theatre work in Germany since 1960 has been done under his old name of Detlef Sierck. He is called Sirk throughout the text.

1918: German Naval Academy, Murwik.

1919: at Munich University (studying law), during the Bavarian Soviet Republic; then to Jena University; switched to philosophy.

1920–22: in Hamburg; one year's newspaper work on the *Neue Hamburger Zeitung*; continued studies at University of Hamburg, switching to the history of art, with Erwin Panofsky; attended Einstein's lectures on relativity. Abandoned University late 1922. His translations of Shakespeare's sonnets published by Verlag Adolf Harms, Hamburg, 1922.

Theatre

[Plays written in German I have given with their German titles and English translations, indicating where the translations may be adaptations. Plays written originally in languages other than English are given solely with their English titles. English plays which have very different, or sometimes unrecognizable, translations in German (*e.g.* Shakespeare's *Twelfth Night*) are given in both languages.]

1920–21 season: Assistant *Dramaturg* at the Deutsches Schauspielhaus, Hamburg.

1921–22 season: *Dramaturg* at the Schauspielhaus, Hamburg.

Probably stayed on at the Hamburg Schauspielhaus for the beginning of the 1922–23 season. September (probably) 1922: staged *Bahnmeister Tod* (*Stationmaster Death*) by Bossdorf.

1922–23 season: Director of the Kleines Theater (Kammerspielbühne), Chemnitz (see p. 17). Staged numerous plays, including: *Tartuffe* (Molière); *Easter* (Strindberg); *Yoschiwara* (Hans Bachwitz); *Madame X* (Alexandre Bisson); *Die Entlassung* (*The Dismissal*, Emil Ludwig); *Versailles* (Emil Ludwig); and works by Georg Büchner, Curt Goetz, *et al.* Also guest director at the Schauspielhaus, Bremen; and staged there at least two plays: *Armand*

Carrel by Moritz Heimann (January 1923) and *Jedermann* (*Everyman*) by Hugo von Hofmannsthal (May 1923).

Summer 1923: staged Ibsen's *Pillars of Society* (with Albert Bassermann in the lead), and *Hamlet* (with Alexander Moissi) at Zoppot Summer Festival.

Autumn 1923–Summer 1929: *Oberspielleiter* (artistic director) at the Schauspielhaus, Bremen. The following is an almost complete list of the plays he staged during this period:

1923–24 season: *The Merry Wives of Windsor* (Shakespeare – translated and adapted by Sirk); *Judith* (Friedrich Hebbel); *Die Freier* (*The Suitors*, Joseph von Eichendorff); *Dream Play* (Strindberg); *Frühlings Erwachen* (Frank Wedekind); *Candida* (Shaw); *Doppelselbstmord* (*Double Suicide*, Ludwig Anzengruber); *Die Kleinen Grossen* (*Man of Destiny/Great Catherine/The Dark Lady of the Sonnets*, Shaw); *Herodes und Mariamne* (*Herod and Mariamne*, Friedrich Hebbel); *Und Pippa Tanzt!* (*And Pippa Dances!*, Gerhart Hauptmann); *Antony and Cleopatra* (Shakespeare); *Die Propheten* (*The Prophets*, Hanns Johst); *The Newly-Married Couple* (Björnstjerne Björnson); *Abschied vom Regiment* (Otto Erich Hartleben); *Medea* (Franz Grillparzer).

1924–25 season: *Kolportage* (Georg Kaiser); *The Doctor's Dilemma* (Shaw); *Vincent* (Hermann Kasack); *Das Kätchen von Heilbronn* (*Little Catherine of Heilbronn*, Kleist); *The Tale of the Wolf* (Franz Molnar); *Saint Joan* (Shaw); *Much Ado About Nothing* (Shakespeare); *Advent* (Strindberg); *Leonarda* (Björnson); *Der Traum Ein Leben* (*Dream is Life*, Franz Grillparzer); *Sakuntala* (Paul Kornfeld – after Kalidasa); *Outward Bound* (*Überfahrt*, Sutton Vane).

1925–26 season: *Caesar and Cleopatra* (Shaw); *Der Kreidekreis* (*The Chalk Circle*, Klabund); *Rheinische Rebellen* (*Rhineland Rebels*, Arnolt Bronnen); *John Gabriel Borkman* (Ibsen); *Madame Sans Gêne* (Victorien Sardou); *Six Characters in Search of an Author* (Luigi Pirandello – trans. and adapted by Sirk); *The Merchant of Venice* (Shakespeare); *Back To Methuselah* – Part I (Shaw); *Napoleon oder Die Hundert Tage* (*Napoleon or the Hundred Days*, Christian Dietrich Grabbe); *Back to Methuselah* – Part II (Shaw); *Der Fröhliche Weinberg* (*The Merry Vineyard*, Carl Zuckmayer); *Juarez und Maximilian* (Franz Werfel); *Liebelei* (*The Reckoning/Playing With Love/Light-o'-Love*, Arthur Schnitzler); *Cyrano de Bergerac* (Edmond Rostand).

1926–27 season: *Weekend* (Noel Coward); *Judith* (Friedrich Hebbel); *Die Räuber* (*The Robbers*, Schiller); *When the Vineyards are in Blossom* (Björnson); *Neithardt von Gneisenau* (Wolfgang Goetz); *The Dictator* (Jules Romains); *Toni* (Gina Kaus); *Cymbeline* (*König Zymbelin*, Shakespeare); *The Barber of Seville* (Beaumarchais); *The Widow of Ephesus* (*Die Witwe von Ephesus*, Lessing); *Man and Superman* (Shaw); *Queen Christina* (Strindberg); *Fanny and the Servant Problem* (Jerome K. Jerome); *Frühlingsopfer* (*Spring's Offering*, Eduard Graf Keyserling).

1927–28 season: *Twelfth Night* (*Dreikönigsnacht*, Shakespeare – adapt. Sirk); *Volpone* (Ben Jonson); *Hermannsschlacht* (*The Battle of Arminius*, Kleist); *The Ringer* (*Der Hexer*, Edgar Wallace); *Lady Windermere's Fan* (Oscar Wilde); *Berenga* (Fred A. Angermayer); *Salome* (Oscar Wilde); *The Shewing-up of Blanco Posnet* (Shaw); *Variété* (Heinrich Mann); *Anatols Hochzeitsmorgen* (*Anatol*, Schnitzler); *Die Jüdin von Toledo* (*The Jewess of Toledo*, Grillparzer – adapt. of *La Judía de Toledo* by Lope de Vega); *Broadway* (George Dunning & Philip Abbott); *Robert Emmet* (Wolfgang Goetz); *Der Turm* (*The Tower*, Hofmannsthal); *At the Gates of the Realm* (Knut Hamsun); *Ein Besserer Herr* (*A Man of Distinction*, Walter Hasenclever); *The Wild Duck* (Ibsen); *Das Kamel Geht Durch Das Nadelöhr* (*The Camel Goes Through the Eye of the Needle*, František Langer).

1928–29 season: *Narziss* (*Narcisse, the Vagrant*, Albert Emil Brachvogel – adapt. James Schönberg); *Oedipus Rex* (Sophocles); *Oktobertag* (*The Phantom Lover*, Georg Kaiser);

Hold Yer Hosses! The Elephants Are Coming (*Hannibal ante Portas*, Robert Sherwood); *As You Like It* (Shakespeare); *Die Dreigroschenoper* (*The Threepenny Opera*, Brecht & Weill); *The Devil's Disciple* (Shaw).

1929–30 season: *Othello* (Shakespeare); *Rivalen* (Carl Zuckmayer – adapt. of *What Price Glory?* by Maxwell Anderson & Laurence Stallings).

Autumn 1929: Sirk was appointed manager (*Direktor*) of the Altes Theater, Leipzig – the city theatre. He held this post until 1936. He was simultaneously artistic director (*Schauspieldirektor*) of the city drama school (*Städtische Schauspielschule*). From 1934, when he entered the cinema and also took on theatre work in Berlin, Sirk did comparatively less work in Leipzig. Among the plays he staged at the Altes Theater, Leipzig, were:

1929–30 season: *Don Carlos* (Schiller); *Im Namen des Volkes!* (*In the Name of the People*, Bernhard Blume).

1930–31 season: *Maria Stuart* (Schiller); *Das Kätchen von Heilbronn* (Kleist); *Der Urfaust* (Goethe); *Faust* (Goethe); *Der Kaiser von Amerika* (*The Applecart*, Shaw).

1931–32 season: *Elizabeth von England* (Bruckner); *Die Ehe* (*The Marriage*, Alfred Döblin); *Liliom* (Molnar); *Monsieur de Pourceaugnac* (Molière); *Twelfth Night* (Shakespeare); *Agnes Bernauer* (Hebbel).

1932–33 season: *Timons Glück und Untergang* (*Timon of Athens*, Shakespeare – much adapt. by Bruckner); *Der Schulze von Zalamea* (*El Alcalde de Zalamea*, Calderón); *Der Silbersee* (*The Silver Lake*, Georg Kaiser).

Dates uncertain: *Wallenstein* (Schiller); *St Joan* (Schiller); *Stille Gäste* (*Silent Guests*, Richard Billinger); *Götz von Berlichingen* (Goethe).

In 1933 Sirk translated and adapted *The Wind and the Rain* (Merton Hodge) as *Regen und Wind*; and in autumn 1934 was invited to stage *Twelfth Night* at the Volksbühne in Berlin. He re-translated the play for this production (see p. 34). He remembers staging only one other play in Berlin: *The Nobel Prize* (Burkmann), presumably at the Volksbühne.

In the summer of 1935, Sirk staged two plays at the Heidelberg Festival: *Der Zerbrochene Krug* (*The Broken Jug*, Kleist), and a medieval play *Lanzelot und Sanderein* (see p. 29).

1936–37 season: Credited as *Spielleiter* at the Komödie, the Komödienhaus Schule, and the Volksbühne, all in Berlin.

1937–38 season: *Spielleiter* at the Komödie, Berlin.

December 1937: Sirk left Germany.

Cinema

Summer 1923: temporary job as a set-designer in Berlin Studio.

1934: hired by Ufa (see p. 34). Began with three short films, all 30–40 min. long, starring Hans H. Schaufuss: one title unknown; *Der Eingebildete Kranke* (*The Imaginary Invalid* based on Molière's *Le Malade Imaginaire*); and *Dreimal Liebe* (*Three Times Love*).

143

Directed

[All opening dates for the German films are for the Berlin premières. Sometimes films were premièred earlier in other cities (e.g. *Schlussakkord* in Dresden), but the reviews in the national press and film magazines appear in the first issue of the respective periodical after the Berlin opening.]

'T was één April [It was in April] (1935)

Production Company	Ufa
Directors	Detlef Sierck, Jacques van Pol

Johan Kaart, Jopie Koopman, Herman Tholen, Cissy van Bennekom, Rob Milton, Tilly Périn-Bouwmeester, Jac. van Bijleveldt, Hilde Alexander.

A baker who has become rich sets up a pasta factory. He is a social climber. A friend decides to play a trick on him, and tells him a baron is going to visit the factory. A fake baron arrives, and is welcomed with a lot of ceremony. The real baron turns up and is thrown out. All ends well.

Dutch language version of *April, April*.

April, April (1935)

Production Company	Ufa
Director	Detlef Sierck
Script	H. W. Litschke, Rudo Ritter
Director of Photography	Willy Winterstein
Music	Werner Bochmann

Carola Höhn (*Friedel*), Albrecht Schoenhals (*The Prince*), Charlotte Daudert (*Mirna*), Lina Carstens (*Mathilde*), Erhard Siedel (*Lampe*), Paul Westermeier (*Fincke*), Hilde Schneider (*Maid*), Annemarie Korff (*Secretary*), Hubert von Meyerinck (*Fake Prince*), Werner Finck, Herbert Weissbach, Wilhelm Egger-Sell, Kurt Felden, Odette Orsy, Josef Reithofer, Wera Schultz, Dorothea Thies.

Opened, Berlin: 24 October 1935. Running time, 82 min.

As *'T was één April*, except that the baron here is a prince.

Das Mädchen vom Moorhof [The Girl from the Marsh Croft] (1935)

Production Company	Ufa
Producer	Peter Paul Brauer
Director	Detlef Sierck
Script	Lothar M. Mayring. From the novel *The Girl from the Marsh Croft* by Selma Lagerlöf
Director of Photography	Willi Winterstein
Editor	Fritz Stapenhorst
Sets	C. L. Kirmse
Music	Hans-Otto Borgmann

Hansi Knoteck (*Helga Christmann*), Ellen Frank (*Gertrud Gerhart*), Kurt Fischer-Fehling (*Karsten Dittmar*), Friedrich Kayssler (*Mr Dittmar*), Eduard von Winterstein (*Mr Gerhart*), Jeanette Bethge (*Mrs Dittmar*), Lina Carstens (*Mrs Christmann*), Franz Stein (*Mr Christmann*), Erwin Klietsch (*Peter Nolde*), Theodor Loos (*Judge*), Fritz Hoopts, Erich Dunskus, Hans Meyer-Hanno, Maria Seidler, Anita Düvel, Ilse Petri, Klaus Pohl, Dorothea Thies, Betty Sedlmayr, Hilde Sessak.

Set among the peat bogs of North Germany. Karsten, a young farmer, is engaged to Gertrud, the daughter of the local potentate, but is really in love with Helga, the girl from the marsh croft. After a drunken brawl in a bar, where a man is killed, Gertrud's family scrap the wedding. Falsity is itself destroyed by social convention. Karsten is free to go off with Helga.

Filmed on location in North Germany, between Bremen and Hamburg. Opened, Berlin: 30 October 1935. Running time, 82 min.

Remade under the same title in 1958 by Gustav Ucicky, with Maria Emo, Claus Holm, Horst Frank.

Stützen der Gesellschaft [Pillars of Society] (1935)

Production Company	R.N. Film der Ufa
Producer	Krüger-Ulrich
Production Manager	Fred Lyssa
Director	Detlef Sierck
Script	Dr Georg C. Klaren, Peter Gillman. From the play *Pillars of Society* by Henrik Ibsen
Director of Photography	Carl Drews
Editor	Friedel Buckow
Sets	O. Gülstorff, H. Minzloff
Music	Franz R. Friedl

Heinrich George (*Consul Bernick*), Maria Krahn (*Betty, his wife*), Horst Teetzmann (*Olaf, his son*), Albrecht Schoenhals (*Johann Tönnessen*), Suse Graf (*Dina Dorf*), Oskar Sima (*Krapp*), Hansjoachim Büttner (*Hammer*), Karl Dannemann (*Aune*), Walter Süssenguth (*Urbini, the Circus Manager*), Paul Beckers (*Hansen, the Clown*), Franz Weber (*Vigeland*), S. O. Schoening (*Sandstadt*), Maria Hofen (*Frau Vigeland*), Tony Tetzlaff (*Frau Sandstadt*), Gerti Ober (*Thora Sandstadt, her daughter*).

Bernick, a rich shipowner in a Norwegian coastal town, has concealed the fact that he is the illegitimate father of Dina. His complacent world is first undermined by the return from the American West of the man in possession of the truth about the past, Johann Tönnessen, who rides into town with a circus. Tönnessen had left many years before, carrying the responsibility for Bernick. Bernick's son, Olaf, stows away on one of his father's ships which is unseaworthy. After a huge storm Bernick dies on the beach, having acknowledged Dina.

Filmed partly on location on the island of Bornholm. Opened, Berlin: 21 December 1935. Running time, 84 min.

Raoul Walsh made a silent version of *Pillars of Society* for Fine Arts in 1916 (which Sirk did not see).

Schlussakkord [Final Accord] (1936)

Production Company	Ufa
Producer	Bruno Duday
Director	Detlef Sierck
Script	Kurt Heuser, Detlef Sierck
Director of Photography	Robert Baberske
Editor	Milo Harbich
Sets	Erich Kettelhut
Music	Kurt Schröder. With parts of Beethoven's *Ninth Symphony*, Tchaikovsky's *Nutcracker Suite*, and Handel's *Judas*, played by the Berliner Solistenvereinigung under the direction of the Berliner Staatsoper.

Willy Birgel (*Garvenberg, the Conductor*), Lil Dagover (*Charlotte, his wife*), Maria von Tasnady (*Hanna*), Theodor Loos (*Dr Obereit*), Maria Koppenhöfer (*Housekeeper*), Albert Lippert (*Clairvoyant*), Kurt Meisel (*Foolish Count*), Erich Ponto (*Chairman of the Assizes*), Peter Bosse, Hella Graf, Paul Otto, Alexander Engel, Eva Tinschmann, Walter Werner, Carl Auen, Erich Bartels, Johannes Bergfeld, Ursula Deinert, Peter Elsholtz, Robert Forsch, Liselotte Köster, Richard Ludwig, Odette Orsy, Hermann Pfeiffer, Ernst Sattler, Walter Steinweg, Bruno Ziener.

'Story has a destitute mother forsake her child to escape to the US with a worthless husband who later shoots himself. Child meantime is adopted by an orchestra conductor, and when the mother returns to Germany she contrives to become its nurse. Eventually the conductor's wife, whose little excursions into illicit amorous affairs get too hot, commits suicide. Blame is thrown on the conductor and the nurse-mother, but they are cleared and marry.' (*Variety*, 16 September 1936).

Opened, Berlin: 24 July 1936. Running time, 101 min.

Sometimes referred to as either *Ninth Symphony* or *Final Accord*. Remade in 1960 by Wolfgang Liebeneiner with the same title.
N.B. Sirk's *Interlude* (1956) is titled *Der Letzte Accord* in Germany.

Das Hofkonzert [The Court Concert] (1936)

Production Company	Ufa
Producer	Bruno Duday
Director	Detlef Sierck
Script	Franz Wallner-Basté, Detlef Sierck. From the play *Das Kleine Hofkonzert* by Paul Verhoeven and Toni Impekoven
Director of Photography	Franz Weihmayr
Sets	Fritz Maurischat
Music	Edmund Nick, Ferenc Vecsey, Robert Schumann

Martha Eggerth (*Christine Holm*), Johannes Heesters (*Walter von Arnegg*), Kurt Meisel (*Florian Schwälbe*), Herbert Hübner (*State Minister*), Ernst Waldow (*Travelling Corset Salesman*), Alfred Abel (*Knips, the Poet*), Hans H. Schaufuss (*Bookworm*), Otto Tressler, Rudolf Klein-Rogge, Flockina von Platen, Hans Richter, Ingeborg von Kusserow, Rudolf Platte, Edwin Jürgensen, Oscar Sabe, Iwa Wanja, Willi Schur, Werner Stock, Toni Tetzlaff,

Gunther Bellier, Johannes Bergfeld, Fritz Berghof, Jac Diehl, Rudolf Essek, Hans Halden, Carl Merznicht, Arnim Süssenguth, Max Vierlinger.

Early nineteenth-century musical romance.

Filmed mainly on location in Würzburg. Opened, Berlin: 12 December 1936. Running time, 85 min.
Remade by Paul Verhoeven in 1944 as *Das Konzert*.

La Chanson du Souvenir [Song of Remembrance] (1936)

Production Company	Ufa
Producer	Bruno Duday
Director	Detlef Sierck
French Supervisor	Serge de Poligny
Dialogue	Georges Neveux. From the play by Paul Verhoeven and Toni Impekoven
Director of Photography	Franz Weihmayr
Music	Edmund Nick
Supervision	Raoul Plequin

Martha Eggerth, Max Michel, Colette Darfeuil, Pierre Magnier, Germaine Laugier, Arvel Boverie, Jean Coquelin, Jean Toulout, Robert Vattier, Marcel Simon, Félix Oudart.

French language version of *Das Hofkonzert*.

Zu Neuen Ufern [Life Begins Anew/To New Shores] (1937)

Production Company	Ufa
Producer	Bruno Duday
Director	Detlef Sierck
Script	Detlef Sierck, Kurt Heuser. Adapted from the novel *Zu Neuen Ufern* by Lovis H. Lorenz
Director of Photography	Franz Weihmayr
Editor	Milo Harbich
Sets	Fritz Maurischat
Music and lyrics	Ralph Benatzky
Costumes	Arno Richter

Zarah Leander (*Gloria Vane*), Willy Birgel (*Sir Albert Finsbury*), Hilde von Stolz (*Fanny, his wife*), Carola Höhn (*Mary, his daughter*), Viktor Staal (*Henry*), Erich Ziegel (*Dr Hoyer*), Edwin Jürgensen (*Governor*), Jakob Tiedtke (*Wells Senior*), Robert Dorsay (*Bobby Wells*), Iwa Wanja (*Violet*), Ernst Legal (*Stout*), Siegfried Schurenberg (*Gilbert*), Lina Lossen (*Head Warden of Paramatta Penitentiary*), Lissi Arna (*Nelly*), Herbert Hübner (*Music-hall Proprietor*), Curd Jürgens.

Gloria Vane, a singer, allows herself to take the rap for her lover, Sir Albert Finsbury, and is sent to Paramatta Penitentiary in Australia. Finsbury, unaware of why she has been deported, moves to Australia to escape his own hopeless situation in England, half-heartedly tries to make contact with Gloria, and ends up marrying the Governor's daughter. Gloria marries a white settler, Henry, to get out of prison but, discovering Finsbury's marriage, despairs; after an unsuccessful stint at night-club singing, she returns 'voluntarily' to Paramatta, whence she is again rescued by the devoted Henry.

Opened, Berlin: 31 August 1937. Running time 106 min.
Shown at Venice Festival, 1937.

Zu Neuen Ufern was titled *Life Begins Anew* by Ufa, but is often referred to as *To New Shores* (the literal translation of the German title).

La Habanera (1937)

Production Company	Ufa
Producer	Bruno Duday
Director	Detlef Sierck
Script	Gerhard Menzel
Director of Photography	Franz Weihmayr
Sets	Anton Weber, Ernst Albrecht
Music	Lothar Brühne
Lyrics: 'Kinderlied', 'Du kannst es nicht wissen'	Detlef Sierck

Zarah Leander (*Astrée Sternhjelm*), Julia Serda (*Ana Sternhjelm*), Ferdinand Marian (*Don Pedro de Avila*), Karl Martell (*Dr Sven Nagel*), Boris Alekin (*Dr Luis Gomez*), Paul Bildt (*Dr Pardway*), Edwin Jürgensen (*Shumann*), Michael Schulz-Dornburg (*Little Juan*), Rosita Alcaraz (*Spanish Dancer*), Lisa Helwig (*Nurse*), Geza von Földessy (*Chauffeur*), Carl Kuhlmann.

On a cruise to Puerto Rico with Ana her aunt, Astrée Sternhjelm falls in love at first sight with a big local landlord, Don Pedro de Avila. She jumps ship and marries him. Ten years later the marriage is on the rocks. Astrée is alone and wretched, hating the sun and the heat, with only her young son for solace. A young Swedish doctor, Dr Sven Nagel, arrives to investigate a mysterious disease on the island. Don Pedro is attempting to cover it up, to protect his fruit trade. At a lavish party, he collapses by his own pool, and Astrée leaves for Sweden with the doctor.

Filmed mainly on location in Tenerife (Spain). Opened, Berlin: 18 December 1937. Running time, 98 min.

Screenplays and projects 1937–38

Sirk wrote several other screenplays at Ufa. Among these were projects based on Faulkner's *Pylon* (later made into *The Tarnished Angels* in Hollywood), Chekhov's *The Shooting Party* (later made into *Summer Storm*), Odön von Horvath's play *Glaube Liebe Hoffnung* (see p. 78). Nabokov's *Laughter in the Dark*, and the Children's Crusade (see p. 108). This last subject was filmed by Andrzej Wajda, 1967, under the title *The Gates of Paradise*.

1937 *Liebling der Matrosen* (director, Hans Hinrich; p.c., Mondial, Vienna; script K. P. Gillmann, Detlef Sierck, from an idea by Rudolf Brettschneider). See p. 52.

1938 *Dreiklang* (director, Hans Hinrich; p.c. Ufa; script, Friedrich Forster-Burggraf, based on an idea by Detlef Sierck from Turgenev's *First Love* and Pushkin's *The Shot*. In fact, Sirk prepared the whole film, including casting, sets, etc.).

Allowed out of Germany to choose locations, presumably in Africa, for a Ufa film *Wiltons Zoo*, Sirk flew to Rome in December 1937, and broke with Ufa and Germany. In early 1938 he wrote a script with his friend Dr Eger for Mondial of Vienna, title unknown. Sirk thinks there was a likelihood of his directing the film, but on the night of 11–12 March the Germans invaded Austria, and it became impossible. In the same year he wrote a script entitled *L'On Revient Toujours*, probably for the French Tobis company: fate unknown. Sirk was asked if he could work on Renoir's *Une Partie de Campagne* (made in 1936) and convert it into a full-length feature. He spent some two months on the project, ultimately leaving the Renoir as it was (see p. 57). (Renoir's masterpiece, precisely because it is not a full-length feature, is currently circulating in Italy in an undifferentiated composite with François Reichenbach's short on the US Marines and the English section of Antonioni's *I Vinti*, under the title of *Fiori della Violenza* [*Flowers of Violence*].)

Accord Final (1939)

Production Company	France Suisse Film
Supervision (uncredited)	Detlef Sierck
Production Manager	Georges Jouanne
Director	I. R. Bay
Script	I. R. Bay, based on his own story
Dialogue	Jacques Natanson
Music	Pasdeloup
Musical Supervisor	Albert Wolff
Violin played by	Zino Francescatti

Kathe de Nagy (*Hélène Vernier/Suzanne Fabre*), Georges Rigaud (*Georges Astor, the Violinist*), Alerme (*Violinist's Manager*), Jules Berry (*Baron Larzac*), Josette Day (*the real Suzanne*), Georges Rollin (*Young Conductor*), Jacques Baumer (*Professor*), Nane Germon.

'A gay-hearted young violin virtuoso, who is noted for his gambling adventures, is led at a drinking party to bet that he will marry within the next two months the tenth girl to enter the music conservatoire on the next morning. He joins the conservatoire incognito as a pupil, and falls in love with the wrong girl . . . who turns out to be the right girl after all' (*Monthly Film Bulletin*).

Filmed in Paris and on Lake Geneva. Running time, 95 min.
Distributor: European (GB).

Boefje (1939)

Production Company	NV City Film
Director	Detlef Sierck
Script	Detlef Sierck and Carl Zuckmayer. From the novel *Boefje* by M. J. Brusse
Director of Photography	Akos Farkas
Editor	Rita Roland

Annie van Ees (*Boefje*), Guus Brox (*Pietje Puck*), Albert von Dalsum (*Priest*).

'Boefje, a boy of sixteen, is a hustler in the sailors' quarter of Rotterdam, along with his friend Pietje Puck. He is spotted by a priest who gets him put into a reformatory. Boefje escapes, and decides to flee to America. With Pietje Puck, he steals money and a map from the priest's house. He repents, but is arrested for a theft he did not commit. After being released he is reconciled with the priest, and decides to begin a new life' (Publicity note).

Filmed in Rotterdam.

Screenplays, short films and projects 1939–43

During the shooting of *Boefje* in Holland, Sirk received a telegram from Warners inviting him to Hollywood to make a new version of *Zu Neuen Ufern*. In Hollywood he re-wrote the story (see p. 60), which Warners then decided not to make. His contract was terminated *circa* 1940.

1941: Made a colour film (*c.* 30–40 min.) on a wine-producing monastery in the Napa Valley (N. California), produced by F. Fromm. (His first use of colour in the cinema.)

Invited to San Francisco light opera company; arrangement collapsed with Pearl Harbor (see p. 61).

1942: Signed writer's contract with Columbia. Scripts include: 1942 *The Date Tree* (not realized as a film); *Malta* (abandoned because it clashed with another Malta project at another studio); 1942–43 *The General's Ring* (based on Selma Lagerlöf's novel of the same name, not made into a film).

About this time Sirk was asked to re-write Robert Wiene's famous 1919 film *The Cabinet of Dr Caligari*. He worked for some months with the owner of the film, Maria Matray. 'I spent about two months on it but it didn't come off. Maria Matray rightly felt, like I did, that it had to be brought up to date. The original is very tied to its time, it is so Expressionist. She wanted me to use the title, and make a psychoanalytic picture out of it. . . . The only thing to do – like with *Atlantis* and *M* – was to write a completely new story' (Sirk). *The Cabinet of Dr Caligari* has since been re-made – by Roger Kay (USA, 1962, with Glynis Johns and Dan O'Herlihy).

Among other projects which Sirk re-proposed were the Children's Crusade and *Laughter in the Dark*; he also suggested a film based on Sherwood Anderson's *Dark Laughter*. At some point during his Columbia period he wrote a script set in a blind people's home – also unrealized (see p. 97). This was also an unrealized project of the late Josef von Sternberg.

Hitler's Madman (1942)

Production Company	Metro-Goldwyn-Mayer
Associate Producer	Rudolph Joseph
Producer	Seymour Nebenzal
Director	Douglas Sirk
Assistant Director	Mel De Lay
Script	Peretz Hirshbein, Melvin Levy, Doris Malloy. From a story by Emil Ludwig and Albrecht Joseph, and *Hangman's Village* by Bart Lytton
Verses	From the poem by Edna St Vincent Millay, 'The Murder of Lidice'
Director of Photography	Jack Greenhalgh [Almost wholly photographed by Eugen Shuftan]
Editor	Dan Milner
Art Directors	Fred Preble, Edward Willens
Music	Karl Hajos

John Carradine (*Heydrich*), Patricia Morison (*Jarmila*), Alan Curtis (*Karel*), Ralph Morgan (*Hanka*), Howard Freeman (*Himmler*), Ludwig Stossel (*Mayor Bauer*), Edgar Kennedy (*Nepomuk*), Jimmy Conlon (*Dvorak*), Blanche Yurka (*Mrs Hanka*), Jorja Rollins (*Clara Janek*), Al Shean (*Priest*), Elizabeth Russell (*Maria*), Victor Kilian (*Janek*), Johanna Hofer (*Mrs Bauer*), Wolfgang Zilzer (*Colonel*), Tully Marshall (*Teacher*), Ava Gardner (*Czech girl terrorized by the Nazis*).

'This story tells of Heydrich's visit to Lidice, his assassination and burning of the village, with the mass-execution of all its male inhabitants. Douglas Sirk originally made the film, but in adding many additional scenes and in "greatly augmenting" the cast, M.G.M. have converted it to a standard cut-to-pattern piece.' (*Monthly Film Bulletin.*)

Filmed in one week in 1942 as an independent production.
Bought by MGM, partly re-shot (October–November 1942) by Sirk. Released in USA, July 1943; GB, 4 October 1943. Running time, 85 min.
Distributors: Loew's Inc (USA); MGM (GB).

Summer Storm (1944)

Production Company	United Artists/Angelus Pictures
Associate Producer	Rudolph Joseph
Producer	Seymour Nebenzal
Production Manager	Walter Mayo
Director	Douglas Sirk
Assistant Director	Bill McGarry
Script	Rowland Leigh, Douglas Sirk. From the adaptation by Douglas Sirk and Michael O'Hara [Douglas Sirk] of *The Shooting Party* by Anton Chekhov
Additional Dialogue	Robert Thoeren
Director of Photography	Archie Stout [In fact, shot almost entirely by Eugen Shuftan.]
Editor	Gregg Tallas
Art Director	Rudi Feld
Music	Karl Hajos
Technical Consultant	Eugen Shuftan
Costumes	Max Pretzfelder

George Sanders (*Fedor Petroff*), Linda Darnell (*Olga*), Anna Lee (*Nadina*), Edward Everett Horton (*Count Volsky*), Hugo Haas (*Urbenin*), Lori Lahner (*Clara*), John Philliber (*Polycarp*), Sig Ruman (*Kuzma*), André Charlot (*Mr Kalenin*), Mary Servoss (*Mrs Kalenin*), John Abbott (*Lunin*), Robert Greig (*Gregory*), Paul Hurst (*Orloff*), Charles Trowbridge (*Doctor*), Byron Foulger (*Clerk in Newspaper Office*), Charles Wagenheim (*Postman*), Frank Orth (*Café Proprietor*), Elizabeth Russell (*Dinner Guest*), Ann Staunton (*Dinner Guest*), Nina Koschetz, Jimmy Conlon, Kate MacKenna, Fred Nurney, Sarah Padden, Sharon McManus, Gabriel Lionoff, Mike Mazurki, Woody Charles, Rex Evans, Kenneth Jones, Anita Venge, Francis Morris.

Shot within a flashback. 'The action takes place in 1912, in pre-revolutionary Russia. The film tells how Olga, married to Urbenin, seduces Count Volsky and Petroff, the judge, before being murdered. A remarkable reconstruction recreates the climate of Russia of the time.... Romantic love scenes prefigure Marylee's reminiscences by the river in *Written on the Wind*, and Reni's flight in *Interlude*. Olga's walk in the woods, her ride with Fedor, the scene where he plays the violin in a cabaret and conducts the orchestra – all these typically Germanic touches are integrated into a Hollywood production style.' (*Cahiers du Cinéma.*)

Filmed December 1943–February 1944. Released in USA, 14 July 1944; GB, 5 February 1945. Running time, 106 min.
Distributors: United Artists (USA and GB).
Assembled and produced by the same group of German emigrés as *Hitler's Madman* (both financed by Brettauer).

Screenplays and projects 1944–45

Cagliostro: based on *Memoirs of a Physician* by Alexandre Dumas, about the legendary doctor-cum-magician-cum-hypnotist. A favourite project of Sirk's, dealing with identity, medicine, sight, and light. A complete screenplay was written, and Sirk had cast George Sanders as Cagliostro and Akim Tamiroff as his sidekick when he abandoned the project. It was later made by Gregory Ratoff, for Edward Small, as *Black Magic* (as far as can be ascertained, based closely on Sirk's original plan). Sirk also planned another film for Edward Small Productions, but this, too, fell through.

A Scandal in Paris (1945)

Production Company	United Artists/Arnold Pressburger Productions Inc.
Associate Producer	Fred Pressburger
Producer	Arnold Pressburger
Director	Douglas Sirk
Assistant Director	Joe Depew
Script	Ellis St Joseph. Based on the *Memoirs* of François Eugène Vidocq
Director of Photography	Guy Roe ['I think I had Shuftan on this picture too' (Sirk)]
Editor	Al Joseph
Art Directors	Gordon Wiles, Frank Sylos
Set Designer	Emile Kuri
Music	Hanns Eisler, Heinz Roemheld
Musical Directors	Hanns Eisler, David Chudnow
Lyrics	Paul Webster

George Sanders (*Vidocq*), Signe Hasso (*Thérèse*), Carol Landis (*Loretta*), Akim Tamiroff (*Emile*), Gene Lockhart (*Richet*), Jo Ann Marlowe (*Mimi*), Alma Kruger (*Marquise*), Alan Napier (*Houdon*), Vladimir Sokoloff (*Uncle Hugo*), Pedro de Cordoba (*Priest*), Leona Maricle (*Owner of Dress Shop*), Fritz Leiber (*Painter*), Skelton Knaggs (*Cousin Pierre*), Fred Nurney (*Cousin Gabriel*), Gisella Werbiseck (*Aunt Ernestine*), Marvin Davis (*Little Louis*).

The life of François Eugène Vidocq, the crook who became the head of the French Sûreté early in the nineteenth century. The film follows his nonchalant progression from jail, via a stint in Napoleon's army (as Lieutenant Rousseau), to the job as head of the police. After infiltrating his crooked colleagues into key posts, and eliminating his only dangerous rival, Vidocq decides to go straight. An almost surrealist film, dense with Sirkian themes – identity, the weight of the past, people as shadows; Vidocq and Emile posing for the painting of St George and the Dragon, the swimming scene, the death on the Chinese carousel – one of Sirk's most delicate works.

Filmed September–December 1945. Released in USA, 19 July 1946; GB, 24 June 1946. Running time, 100 min.
Distributors: United Artists (USA and GB).
Current GB Distributor: Watsofilms Ltd (16 mm).

Lured/Personal Column (1946)

Production Company	United Artists/Oakmont Pictures
Executive Producer	Hunt Stromberg
Associate Producers	James Nasser, Henry Kesler
Director	Douglas Sirk
Assistant Director	Clarence Eurist
Script	Leo Rosten. From a story by Jacques Campaneez, Ernest Neuville, Simon Gantillon
Dialogue Director	Stuart Hall
Director of Photography	William Daniels
Editors	James E. Newcom, John M. Foley
Art Director	Nicolai Remisoff
Music	Michel Michelet

George Sanders (*Robert Fleming*), Lucille Ball (*Sandra Carpenter*), Charles Coburn (*Inspector Temple*), Boris Karloff (*Artist*), Sir Cedric Hardwicke (*Julian Wilde*), Alan Mowbray (*Maxwell*), George Zucco (*Officer Barrett*), Joseph Calleia (*Dr Moryani*), Tania Chandler (*Lucy Barnard*), Alan Napier (*Gordon*), Robert Coote (*Policeman*), Sam Harris (*Old Man at Concert asking for whisky*).

Sandra Carpenter agrees to go to work for the vice squad in London in the early days of the century to try and trap a white-slaver (who is an admirer of Baudelaire). As in *Scandal in Paris*, a zany world of appearances, deceit, money, and boredom. The last of Sirk's independently produced films during his first period in America. Leo Rosten and Sirk re-wrote for this film the screenplay of *Pièges* (*Snares/Personal Column*) directed by Robert Siodmak in 1939, with Maurice Chevalier, Marie Dea, Pierre Renoir, and Erich von Stroheim.

Filmed October–December 1946. Released in USA, September 1947; GB, 9 February 1948. Running time, 102 min.
Distributors: United Artists (USA and GB).

1947 *Siren of Atlantis/Atlantis, the Lost Continent* (direction credited to G. Tallas; some direction probably by Arthur Ripley and (perhaps) John Brahm; script by Rowland Leigh, Robert Lax, and [uncredited] Douglas Sirk, from the novel by Pierre Benoit). An attempted re-make of Pabst's *Die Herrin von Atlantis* (1932). Sirk thinks he did some writing, but no direction (see p. 75). Benoit's famous novel has been filmed at least four times: in 1913, 1932 (Pabst), 1948 (Ripley) and 1961 (Ulmer).

Sleep, My Love (1947)

Production Company	United Artists/Triangle
Associate Producer	Harold Greene
Producers	(For Mary Pickford/Triangle) Charles Buddy Rogers, Ralph Cohn
Production Manager	Robert Bache
Director	Douglas Sirk
Assistant Director	Clarence Eurist
Script	St Clair McKelway, Leo Rosten. From a story by Leo Rosten
Director of Photography	Joseph Valentine
Camera Operator	Edward Coleman

* *Lured* was re-titled *Personal Column* during the run (see p. 75).

153

Editor	Lynn Harrison
Art Director	William Ferrari
Set Designer	Howard Bristol
Music	David Chudnow
Musical Director	Rudy Schrager
Script Supervisor	Mary Gibson Whitlock
Costumes	Margaret Jennings
Gowns	Sophie

Claudette Colbert (*Alison Courtland*), Robert Cummings (*Bruce Elcott*), Don Ameche (*Richard Courtland*), Rita Johnson (*Barby*), George Coulouris (*Charles Vernay*), Hazel Brooks (*Daphne*), Keye Luke (*Jimmie*), Fred Nurney (*Haskins*), Ralph Morgan (*Dr Rhinehart*), Queenie Smith (*Mrs Vernay*), Maria San Marco (*Jeannie*), Anne Triola (*Waitress*), Lilian Bronson (*Helen*), Raymond Burr (*Lieutenant Strake*), Lillian Randolph.

'Don Ameche wants to get rid of his wife, Claudette Colbert. As is right, Robert Cummings prevents this taking place. Sirk's attention is focused almost entirely on Claudette Colbert' (*Cahiers du Cinéma*). 'The *Cahiers* are quite right, that's all there was that I could do' (Sirk). One can, however, note the theme of blindness, the use of photography, screens, frosted glass; the antithesis of house and garden (conservatory). Hazel Brooks is striking as Daphne, Ameche's mistress.

Filmed May–August 1947. Released in USA, January 1948; GB, 1 November 1948. Running time, 90 min.
Distributors: United Artists (USA and GB).
Current GB Distributor: Robert Kingston Films (16 mm).

Slightly French (1948)

Production Company	Columbia
Producer	Irving Starr
Production Manager	Jack Fier
Director	Douglas Sirk
Assistant Director	Paul Donnelly
Script	Karen de Wolf. From a story by Herbert Fields
Script Supervisor	Rose Loewinger
Director of Photography	Charles Lawton
Editor	Al Clark
Art Director	Carl Anderson
Set Designer	James Crowe
Musical Directors	George Duning, Morris Stoloff
Lyrics	Allan Roberts, Lester Lee
Choreography	Robert Sidney
Gowns	Jean Louis

Dorothy Lamour (*Mary O'Leary*), Don Ameche (*John Gayle*), Janis Carter (*Louisa Hide*), Willard Parker (*Doug Hide*), Adèle Jurgens (*Latour, French Actress*), Jeanne Manet (*Nicolette*), Patricia White (*Hilda*), Frank Ferguson, Myron Healey, Leonard Carey, Earle Hodgins.

A film director, John Gayle, is fired for his slave-driving methods. The star of the film has given up in despair. The film needs a French star. Gayle finds Bowery-born Mary O'Leary in a carnival on Coney Island; he grooms her in secret, and springs her on the producer, Doug Hide. Gayle is reinstated until Mary explodes without her French accent. He is fired again, but Mary is now in love with him and he has to be brought back to finish the film.

Filmed January–February 1948. Released in USA, February 1949; GB, December 1948. Running time, 81 min.
Distributors: Columbia (USA and GB).

Shockproof (1948)

Production Company	Columbia
Associate Producer	Earl McEvoy
Producers	S. Sylvan Simon, Helen Deutsch
Production Manager	Jack Fier
Director	Douglas Sirk
Assistant Director	Earl Bellamy
Script	Helen Deutsch, Samuel Fuller
Script Supervisor	Rose Loewinger
Director of Photography	Charles Lawton
Camera Operator	Vic Schurich
Editor	Gene Havlick
Art Director	Carl Anderson
Set Designer	Louis Diage
Music	George Duning
Musical Director	Morris Stoloff
Gowns	Jean Louis

Cornel Wilde (*Griff Marat*), Patricia Knight (*Jenny Marsh*), John Baragrey (*Harry Wesson*), Esther Minciotti (*Mrs Marat*), Howard St John (*Sam Brooks*), Russell Collins (*Frederick Bauer*), Charles Bates (*Tommy Marat*), Gilbert Barnett (*Barry*), Frank Jaquet (*Monte*), Frank Ferguson (*Logan*), Ann Shoemaker (*Dr Daniels*), King Donovan (*Joe Wilson*), Claire Carleton (*Florrie Kobiski*), Al Eben (*Joe Kobiski*).

Jenny Marsh is released on parole after serving 5 years of a life sentence for murder. Her parole officer, Griff Marat, gives her a job in his house looking after his blind mother. He is in with the local politicians, and is keen on promotion. Jenny is under an injunction not to see her old lover, Harry Wesson; she falls in love with Griff, and they marry, but when Wesson threatens her, she accidentally shoots him, and both she and Griff run away. After living in hiding, they decide to return and give themselves up. A trick happy ending, forced on Sirk, has Wesson only slightly injured, and he does not even make a charge.

Filmed June–July 1948. Released in USA, January 1949; GB, 27 June 1949. Running time, 80 min.
Distributors: Columbia (USA and GB).

1948 *Lulu Belle* (director Leslie Fenton; script by Everett Freeman; p.c., Columbia; based on the play by Charles MacArthur and Edward Sheldon, with additional dialogue by Karl Lamb; starring Dorothy Lamour and George Montgomery). Credited to Sirk in some sources. 'I think I did some writing on it, and perhaps some direction. But I'm not sure, and I'm not interested in these patchwork things' (Sirk).

After this Sirk left Hollywood and returned to Germany (1949–50). His contract with Columbia was terminated, at his request.

1950 On his return to America from Germany, Seymour Nebenzal asked Sirk to re-write and re-make the famous Lang film, *M.* Sirk wrote a new script, but declined to direct the kind of thing Nebenzal had in mind (see p. 82).

The First Legion (1950)

Production Company	United Artists/Sedif Pictures Corporation
Producers	Douglas Sirk, Rudolph Joseph
Director	Douglas Sirk
Script	Emmet Lavery. Adapted from his play *The First Legion*
Director of Photography	Robert de Grasse
Editor	Francis D. Lyon
Music	Hans Sommer
Technical Consultant	Father Thomas J. Sullivan of the University of St Ignatius Loyola

Charles Boyer (*Father Marc Arnoux*), William Demarest (*Monsignor Michael Carey*), Lyle Bettger (*Dr Peter Morrell*), Barbara Rush (*Terry Gilmartin*), Leo G. Carroll (*Father Paul Duquesne*), Walter Hampden (*Father Edward Quarterman*), Wesley Addy (*Father John Fulton*), Taylor Holmes (*Father Keene*), H. B. Warner (*Father José Sierra*), George Zucco (*Father Robert Stuart*), John McGuire (*Father Tom Rawleigh*), Clifford Brooke (*Lay Brother*), Dorothy Adams (*Mrs Dunn*), Molly Lamont (*Mrs Gilmartin*), Queenie Smith (*Henrietta*), Jacqueline de Wit (*Nurse*), Bill Edwards (*Joe*).

Father Marc Arnoux, an ex-criminal attorney, is the head of a Jesuit seminary full of such unlikely priests as Father John Fulton, a former concert pianist, uncertain whether to remain in the order or leave and pursue his music. The ailing Father José Sierra suddenly regains the use of his legs – but this 'miracle' has been accomplished by the local doctor, Dr Peter Morrell, an agnostic. The film then moves on to its climax, a 'real' miracle, in which crippled Terry Gilmartin rises from her wheelchair. Numerous themes dear to Sirk: religion and the absurd; the relationship between the 'rational' and the 'irrational', and the narrow (or non-existent) borderline between the two.

Filmed as an independent production on location at the Mission Inn, Riverside, May–June 1950. Released in USA, 11 May 1951; GB, 17 September 1951. Running time, 86 min. Distributors: United Artists (USA and GB).

Mystery Submarine (1950)

Production Company	Universal International
Producer	Ralph Dietrich
Director	Douglas Sirk
Assistant Directors	Milton Carter, Charles Bennett
Second Unit	Frank Shaw
Script	Ralph Dietrich, George W. George. From a story by George W. George and George F. Slavin
Director of Photography	Clifford Stine
Special Effects	David S. Horsley
Editor	Virgil Vogel
Art Directors	Bernard Herzbrun, Robert Boyle
Set Designers	Russell A. Gausman, Otto Siegel

Music	Joseph Gershenson
Costumes	Bill Thomas
Technical Consultant	Commander B. R. van Buskirk

Macdonald Carey (*Brett Young*), Marta Toren (*Madeline Brenner*), Robert Douglas (*Commander von Molter*), Carl Esmond (*Heldman*), Ludwig Donath (*Dr Adolph Guernitz*), Jacqueline Dalya Hilliard (*Carla*), Fred Nurney (*Bruno*), Katharine Warren (*Mrs Weber*), Howard Negley (*Captain Elliott*), Bruce Morgan (*Kramer*), Ralph Brooker (*Stefan*), Paul Hoffman (*Hartwig*), Peter Michael, Larry Winter, Frank Rawls, Peter Similuk (*Members of the Crew*), Lester Sharpe (*Citadel Captain*), Jimmy Best (*Navy Lieutenant*).

Sirk's first assignment at Universal. Weighed down by a poor story and a cast headed by Macdonald Carey, who plays Brett Young, a US under-cover agent who has been infiltrated on to a German submarine, kidnapping Dr Adolph Guernitz, an important scientist. 'I can remember nothing about many of the early Universal pictures, and anyway, they are best forgotten' (Sirk).

Filmed July–September 1950. Released in USA, December 1950; GB, 22 January 1951. Running time, 78 min.
Distributors: Universal (USA), GFD (GB).

Thunder on the Hill (1951)

Production Company	Universal International
Producer	Michel Kraike
Production Manager	E. Dodds
Director	Douglas Sirk
Assistant Director	John Sherwood
Script	Oscar Saul, Andrew Solt. From the play *Bonaventure* by Charlotte Hastings
Director of Photography	William Daniels
Editor	Ted J. Kent
Art Directors	Bernard Herzbrun, Nathan Juran
Set Designers	Russell A. Gausman, John Austin
Music	Hans J. Salter
Costumes	Bill Thomas

Claudette Colbert (*Sister Mary Bonaventure*), Ann Blyth (*Valerie Carns*), Robert Douglas (*Dr Jeffreys*), Anne Crawford (*Isabel Jeffreys*), Philip Friend (*Sidney Kingham*), Gladys Cooper (*Mother Superior*), Michael Pate (*Willy*), John Abbott (*Abel Harmer*), Gavin Muir (*Melling*), Connie Gilchrist (*Sister Josephine*), Phyllis Stanley (*Nurse Phillips*), Norma Varden (*Pierce*), Valerie Cardew (*Nurse Colby*), Queenie Leonard (*Mrs Smithson*), Patrick O'Moore (*Mr Smithson*).

'A flood in the county of Norfolk forces the inhabitants to take refuge in a convent nearby. Ann Blyth, who is under sentence of death for the murder of her brother, is among those fleeing the flood. Sister Mary Bonaventure (Claudette Colbert) becomes attached to Ann Blyth, and discovers the truth – that she is innocent. Somewhat hampered by the script, which is a mixture of religious police intrigue and metaphysical drama, Sirk finds in this extreme psychological climate, among the unleashed elements, the exact sense of melodrama' (*Cahiers du Cinéma*). Contrary to some suggestions, *Thunder on the Hill* has no affiliation to Bresson's *Les Anges du Péché*.

Filmed November–December 1950. Released in USA, September 1951; GB, 25 June 1951.
Running time, 84 min.
Distributors: Universal (USA), GFD (GB).
GB title: *Bonaventure*.

The Lady Pays Off (1951)

Production Company	Universal International
Producer	Albert J. Cohen
Production Manager	A. Mack d'Agostino
Director	Douglas Sirk
Assistant Director	Fred Frank
Script	Frank Gill Jr, Albert J. Cohen
Director of Photography	William Daniels
Special Effects	David S. Horsley
Editor	Russell Schoengarth
Art Directors	Bernard Herzbrun, Robert Boyle
Set Designers	Russell A. Gausman, Julia Heron
Music	Frank Skinner
Costumes	Bill Thomas

Linda Darnell (*Evelyn Warren*), Stephen McNally (*Matt Braddock*), Gigi Perreau (*Diana Braddock*), Virginia Field (*Kay Stoddard*), Ann Codee (*Marie*), Lynne Hunter (*Minnie*), Nestor Paiva (*Manuel*).

Evelyn Warren, who has just been chosen as America's 'Teacher of the Year', goes to Reno, gets drunk and loses 7,000 dollars in Matt Braddock's casino. He threatens to give the story to the press, but in return for not doing so pressures her into tutoring his daughter Diana. Evelyn decides to make him fall for her, succeeds, and then leaves. The child wins her back. 'I have no feeling for this picture at all' (Sirk).

Filmed April–May 1951. Released in USA, November 1951; GB, 5 November 1951. Running time, 80 min.
Distributors: Universal (USA), GFD (GB).

Weekend with Father (1951)

Production Company	Universal International
Producer	Ted Richmond
Production Manager	A. Mack d'Agostino
Director	Douglas Sirk
Assistant Director	Fred Frank
Script	Joseph Hoffman. From a story by George F. Slavin and George W. George
Director of Photography	Clifford Stine
Editor	Russell Schoengarth
Art Directors	Bernard Herzbrun, Robert Boyle
Set Designers	Russell A. Gausman, Ruby R. Levitt
Music	Frank Skinner
Costumes	Bill Thomas

158

Van Heflin (*Brad Stubbs*), Patricia Neal (*Jean Bowen*), Gigi Perreau (*Anne Stubbs*), Virginia Field (*Phyllis Reynolds*), Richard Denning (*Don Adams*), Jimmy Hunt (*Gary Bowen*), Janine Perreau (*Patty Stubbs*), Tommy Rettig (*David Bowen*), Gary Pagett (*Eddie Lewis*), Frances Williams (*Cleo*), Elvia Allman (*Mrs G.*).

A widower, Brad Stubbs, and a widow, Jean Bowen, meet while sending their children off to camp. He is being pursued by a glamorous TV star, whom his daughters would like him to marry; she is pursued by a nature-boy PT instructor, whom her sons would like her to marry. 'It has the Thoreau theme in it; it ties up with *All That Heaven Allows*. . . . I can't remember the picture too well any longer. I think I did it only for the children' (Sirk).

Filmed June–July 1951. Released in USA, December 1951; GB, 14 January 1952. Running time, 83 min.
Distributors: Universal (USA), GFD (GB).

Has Anybody Seen My Gal? (1951)

Production Company	Universal International
Producer	Ted Richmond
Director	Douglas Sirk
Script	Joseph Hoffman. Based on a story by Eleanor H. Porter
Director of Photography	Clifford Stine
Colour Process	Technicolor
Colour Consultant	William Fritzsche
Editor	Russell Schoengarth
Art Directors	Bernard Herzbrun, Hilyard Brown
Set Designers	Russell A. Gausman, John Austin
Music	Joseph Gershenson
Lyrics:	
'Five Foot Two, Eyes of Blue'	sung by College Boys and Girls
'When the Red, Red Robin Comes Bob-Bob-Bob-bin' Along'	sung by Charles Coburn, Gigi Perreau, Lynn Bari
'Gimme a Little Kiss, Will Ya, Huh?'	sung by Piper Laurie
'It Ain't Gonna Rain No More'	sung by Charles Coburn and Group
'Tiger Rag'	played by Group
Choreography	Harold Belfer
Titles	John Held Jr.
Gowns	Rosemary Odell

Charles Coburn (*Samuel Fulton*), Piper Laurie (*Millicent Blaisdell*), Rock Hudson (*Dan Stebbins*), Gigi Perreau (*Roberta Blaisdell*), Frank Ferguson (*Edward Norton*), Skip Homeier (*Carl Pennock*), Natalie Schafer (*Clarissa Pennock*), Paul Harvey (*Judge Wilkins*), Forrest Lewis (*Quinn*), Lynn Bari (*Harriet Blaisdell*), Larry Gates (*Charles Blaisdell*), William Reynolds (*Howard Blaisdell*), James Dean (*Ice-cream Lover*).

Samuel Fulton, posing as an eccentric artist, takes a room in the house of the Blaisdell family. Mr Blaisdell is the son of the woman Fulton nearly married, before he became a multi-millionaire. He now wants to see if they will be all right to leave his fortune to. He passes them

159

100,000 dollars anonymously, with disastrous effects, especially on Mrs Blaisdell, who insists on moving into a vast mansion, and tries to marry her daughter Millicent off to a pretentious young man, instead of her previous boyfriend Dan Stebbins, who is a soda jerk. After various set-backs they happily return to their old house, and Fulton departs confident they can now take the fortune. (Sirk's first colour feature.)

Filmed October–November 1951. Released in USA, July 1952; GB, 23 June 1952. Running time, 89 min.
Distributors: Universal (USA), GFD (GB).

No Room For The Groom (1952)

Production Company	Universal International
Producer	Ted Richmond
Production Manager	Jack Gertsman
Director	Douglas Sirk
Assistant Directors	Fred Frank, George Lollier
Script	Joseph Hoffman. Based on the novel *My True Love* by Darwin L. Teilhet
Dialogue Director	Jack Daniels
Director of Photography	Clifford Stine
Editor	Russell Schoengarth
Art Directors	Bernard Herzbrun, Richard H. Riedel
Set Designers	Russell A. Gausman, Ruby R. Levitt
Music	Frank Skinner
Costumes	Bill Thomas

Tony Curtis (*Alvah Morell*), Piper Laurie (*Lee Kingshead*), Don de Fore (*Herman Strouple*), Spring Byington (*Mama*), Jack Kelly (*Will Stubbins*), Lee Aaker (*Donovan*), Lillian Bronson (*Elsa*), Stephen Chase (*Mr Taylor*), Paul McVey (*Dr Trotter*), Lynn Hunter (*Cousin Betty*), Fess Parker (*Cousin Ben*), Frank Sully (*Cousin Luke*), Helen Noyes (*Cousin Emmy*), Elsie Baker (*Cousin Julia*), Fred J. Miller (*Cousin Henry*), James Parnell (*Cousin Mike*), Lee Turnbull (*Cousin Pete*), Janet Clark (*Cousin Dorothy*), Dolores Mann (*Cousin Susie*), Alice Rickey (*Cousin Kate*).

A GI, Alvah Morrell, who has eloped to Las Vegas to marry his girl-friend, Lee Kingshead, returns from Korea to find she has not told her family of the wedding. The house is crammed with relatives, including Laurie's fearsome mother who is determined to marry her off to a rich cement tycoon, who is anyway trying to run a railway through the house. 'I think I had to do it as a tryout for Tony Curtis ... I can remember nothing about this picture at all' (Sirk).

Filmed January–February 1952. Released in USA, May 1952; GB, 4 August 1952. Running time, 82 min.
Distributors: Universal (USA), GFD (GB).

Meet Me at the Fair (1952)

Production Company	Universal International
Producer	Albert J. Cohen
Production Manager	Arthur Siteman
Director	Douglas Sirk
Assistant Directors	Fred Frank, Phil Bowles

Script	Irving Wallace. From the adaptation by Martin Berkeley of *The Great Companions* by Gene Markey
Dialogue Director	Jack Daniels
Director of Photography	Maury Gertsman
Colour Process	Technicolor
Colour Consultant	William Fritzsche
Editor	Russell Schoengarth
Art Directors	Bernard Herzbrun, Eric Orbom
Set Designers	Russell A. Gausman, Ruby R. Levitt
Music	Joseph Gershenson
Lyrics:	
'Meet Me at the Fair'	Milton Rosen, Frederick Herbert; sung by Carole Mathews
'I Was There'	F. E. Miller, Benjamin 'Scat Man' Crothers; sung by Dan Dailey, 'Scat Man' Crothers, and Chet Allen
'Remember the Time'	Kenny Williams, Marvin Wright; sung by Dan Dailey and Carole Mathews
'Ave Maria'	Franz Schubert; sung by Chet Allen
'Ezekiel Saw de Wheel'	sung by 'Scat Man' Crothers
'Sweet Genevieve'	George Cooper, Henry Tucker; sung by the Quartette
'All God's Chillun Got Wings'	sung by 'Scat Man' Crothers and Chet Allen
'I Got the Shiniest Mouth in Town'	Stan Freeburg; sung by 'Scat Man' Crothers
'O Susannah!'	Stephen Foster; sung by Dan Dailey, 'Scat Man' Crothers, and Chet Allen
'Bill Bailey, Won't You Please Come Home?'	Hughie Cannon; sung by Carole Mathews
Choreography	Kenny Williams
Costumes	Rosemary Odell

Dan Dailey (*'Doc' Tilbee*), Diana Lynn (*Zerelda Wing*), Hugh O'Brien (*Chilton Corr*), Carole Mathews (*Clara Brink*), 'Scat Man' Crothers (*Enoch Jones*), Rhys Williams (*Pete McCoy*), Russell Simpson (*Sheriff Evans*), Franklin Farnum (*Himself*), Roger Moore (*Himself*), Harte Wayne (*Himself*), Chet Allen (*'Tad' Bayliss*), 'Iron Eyes' Cody (*Chief Rain-in-the-Face*), Thomas E. Jackson (*Billy Gray*), George Chandler (*Deputy Sheriff Leach*), Doris Packer (*Mrs Swaile*), Robert Shafto (*Prime Minister Disra*), John Maxwell (*Mr Spooner*), Virginia Brissac (*Mrs Spooner*), George L. Spaulding (*Governor*), Butch (the dog *Spook*).

See p. 87 for description.

Filmed May–June 1952. Released in USA, January 1953; GB, 22 June 1953. Running time, 87 min.
Distributors: Universal (USA), GFD (GB).

Take Me to Town (1952)

Production Company	Universal International
Producers	Leonard Goldstein, Ross Hunter
Production Manager	Edward Dodds
Director	Douglas Sirk
Assistant Directors	Joseph E. Kenny, Gordon McLean
Script	Richard Morris. From his story *Flame of Timberline*

Dialogue Director	Jack Daniels
Director of Photography	Russell Metty
Colour Process	Technicolor
Colour Consultant	William Fritzsche
Editor	Milton Carruth
Art Directors	Bernard Herzbrun, Hilyard Brown, Alexander Golitzen
Set Designers	Russell A. Gausman, Julia Heron
Music	Joseph Gershenson
Lyrics:	
'Oh, You Red-Head'	Frederick Herbert, Milton Rosen; sung by Ann Sheridan, Lee Patrick, and chorus
'Take Me to Town'	Lester Lee, Dan Shapiro; sung by the Pickett Sisters
'The Tale of Vermilion O'Toole'	Frederick Herbert; sung by Dusty Walker
'Holy, Holy, Holy'	sung by a choir
Choreography	Hal Belfer
Costumes	Bill Thomas

Ann Sheridan (*Vermilion O'Toole*), Sterling Hayden (*Will Hall*), Philip Reed (*Newton Cole*), Phyllis Stanley (*Mrs Stoffer*), Larry Gates (*Ed Daggett*), Lee Patrick (*Rose*), Forrest Lewis (*Ed Higgins*), Lee Aaker (*Corney Hall*), Ann Tyrell (*Louise Pickett*), Dorothy Neumann (*Felice Pickett*), Robert Anderson (*Chuck*), Frank Sully (*Sammy*), Harvey Grant (*Petey Hall*), Dusty Henley (*Bucket Hall*), Robert Anderson (*Chuck*), Lane Chandler (*Mike*), The Pickett Sisters.

Will Hall is a widower living in the backwoods with his three sons, and is part-time preacher for the local community. Vermilion O'Toole is 'a woman with a past' on the run from the law. Hall's sons think she would make a good wife for him. She kills a bear, scares off an old lover from the past, raises money for the church, and ends up giving Bible classes.

Filmed October–November 1952. Released in USA, June 1953; GB, 5 October 1953. Running time, 80 min.
Distributors: Universal (USA), GFD (GB).

All I Desire (1953)

Production Company	Universal International
Producer	Ross Hunter
Production Manager	A. Mack d'Agostino
Director	Douglas Sirk
Assistant Directors	Joseph E. Kenny, Ronnie Rondell
Script	James Gunn, Robert Blees. From the novel *Stopover* by Carol Brink, adapted by Gina Kaus
Dialogue Director	Jack Daniels
Director of Photography	Carl Guthrie
Editor	Milton Carruth
Art Directors	Bernard Herzbrun, Alexander Golitzen
Set Designers	Russell A. Gausman, Julia Heron
Music	Joseph Gershenson
Lyric:	
'All I Desire'	David Lieber
Choreography	Kenny Williams
Costumes	Rosemary Odell

Barbara Stanwyck (*Naomi Murdoch*), Richard Carlson (*Henry Murdoch*), Lyle Bettger (*Dutch Heineman*), Marcia Henderson (*Joyce Murdoch*), Maureen O'Sullivan (*Sara Harper*), Richard Long (*Russ Underwood*), Fred Nurney (*Peterson*), Billy Gray (*Ted Murdoch*), Lotte Stein (*Lena Engstrom*), Lori Nelson (*Lily Murdoch*), Dayton Lummis (*Colonel Underwood*), Lela Bliss (*Belle Staley*), Ed Cobb (*Driver*), Henry Hoople (*Dutch Heineman's Customer*), Guy Williams, Charles Hand.

Naomi returns to the Wisconsin town she left many years before, to see one of her daughters acting in the school play. Her husband Henry welcomes her back, as does her old lover, Dutch Heineman – with whom she has broken. A study of the American family and of small-town life. Hints at reactionary pressures in education (the figure of Colonel Underwood); small-town gossip. The 'liberated' zone of the house is the kitchen.

Filmed December 1952–January 1953. Released in USA, July 1953; GB, 22 June 1953. Running time, 79 min.
Distributors: Universal (USA), GFD (GB).

Taza, Son of Cochise (1953)

Production Company	Universal International
Producer	Ross Hunter
Director	Douglas Sirk
Assistant Director	Tom Shaw
Script	George Zuckerman. Adapted by Gerald Drayson Adams from his own story
Director of Photography	Russell Metty (3-D)
Colour Process	Technicolor
Colour Consultant	William Fritzsche
Editor	Milton Carruth
Art Directors	Bernard Herzbrun, Emrich Nicholson
Set Designers	Russell A. Gausman, Oliver Emert
Music	Frank Skinner
Costumes	Jay A. Morley Jr.

Rock Hudson (*Taza*), Barbara Rush (*Oona*), Gregg Palmer (*Captain Burnett*), Bart Roberts (*Naiche*), Morris Ankrum (*Grey Eagle*), Eugene Iglesias (*Chato*), Richard H. Cutting (*Cy Hagen*), Ian MacDonald (*Geronimo*), Joe Sawyer (*Sergeant Hamma*), Lance Fuller (*Lieutenant Willis*), Brad Jackson (*Lieutenant Richards*), Robert Burton (*General Crook*), Charles Horvath (*Locha*), James van Horn (*Skinya*), Robert Hoy (*Lobo*), Barbara Burck (*Location Bit*), Dan White (*Charlie*), Jeff Chandler as the dying Cochise.

'One of Sirk's most beautiful films. The action sequences have the punch of Mann's most effective films, the description of the Indian camp and the customs of its inhabitants make one think of the Daves of *Broken Arrow* through its perfection and its humanism, but it is above all in the scenes of intimacy that Sirk's talent is most apparent. Out of one scene between Rock Hudson and Barbara Rush he makes a wonderful poem of love, and when the action becomes more precise . . . it is to the purest sense of the *tragic* that he appeals. . . . Sirk makes sublime a scene which the dialogue was beginning to make mediocre, and with a detail, the beauty of a gesture, or a look from the wonderful Barbara Rush he recovers his sense of lyricism. Is not the summit of the film that overwhelming scene where Rock Hudson finds the marks of the lash on the naked back of Barbara Rush?' (P.B. in *Le Western*.)

Taza, Sirk's first script with Zuckerman, sometimes attacked by his admirers, needs to be rescued from the categorization of a reactionary Western. In fact, the character of Taza himself fits into the in-between group Sirk talks about. Taza is a compromiser, because he is caught in between two opposing groups – the US Army and the 'left-wing' Indians, led by his brother. In such a situation, he argues for 'peaceful co-existence'.

Filmed on location in Utah, mainly near Moab, July–August 1953. Released in USA, February 1954; GB, 17 May 1954. Running time, 77 min.
Distributors: Universal (USA), GFD (GB).

Magnificent Obsession (1953)

Production Company	Universal International
Producer	Ross Hunter
Director	Douglas Sirk
Second Unit	James C. Havens
Assistant Directors	William Holland, Gordon McLean
Script	Robert Blees. From the novel by Lloyd C. Douglas and the script by Sarah Y. Mason and Victor Heerman, adapted by Wells Root
Director of Photography	Russell Metty
Colour Process	Technicolor
Colour Consultant	William Fritzsche
Special Effects	David S. Harsley
Editor	Milton Carruth
Art Directors	Bernard Herzbrun, Emrich Nicholson
Set Designers	Russell A. Gausman, Ruby R. Levitt
Costumes	Bill Thomas

Jane Wyman (*Helen Phillips*), Rock Hudson (*Bob Merrick*), Agnes Moorhead (*Nancy Ashford*), Otto Kruger (*Randolph*), Barbara Rush (*Joyce Phillips*), Gregg Palmer (*Tom Masterson*), Sara Shane (*Valerie*), Paul Cavanagh (*Dr Giraud*), Judy Nugent (*Judy*), George Lynn (*Williams*), Richard H. Cutting (*Dr Dodge*), Robert B. Williams (*Sergeant Burnham*), Helen Kleeb (*Mrs Eden*), Fred Nurney (*Doctor*), Will White (*Sergeant Ames*).

A worthless playboy is saved from death after a boating accident by the respirator kept nearby for an ailing doctor. At the same time, the doctor has a collapse and dies. Merrick is hospitalized in the dead doctor's clinic (Brightwood). After breaking out of the hospital, he is given a lift into town by the doctor's widow; Merrick first discovers who she is – and she then discovers who he is. After some drinking, Merrick decides to return to medicine, which he had earlier abandoned. He contacts Helen under a false name after she has been made blind from an accident due to his importuning her in a taxi. They fall in love. After much ill fortune, Merrick cures her at death's door.

An appalling weepie, remarkable for Sirk's stunning direction. Numerous demonstrations of lighting, camerawork, music – in short, style – redeem an otherwise atrocious tale. Re-make of John Stahl's *Magnificent Obsession* (1935), with Irene Dunn, Robert Taylor, Charles Butterworth.

Filmed September–October 1953. Released in USA, August 1954; GB, 20 December 1954. Running time, 108 min.
Distributors: Universal (USA), GFD (GB).

Sign of the Pagan (1954)

Production Company	Universal International
Producer	Albert J. Cohen
Director	Douglas Sirk
Second Unit	James C. Havens
Assistant Directors	John Sherwood, Marshall Green, George Lollier
Script	Oscar Brodney, Barre Lyndon
Director of Photography	Russell Metty (Cinemascope)
Colour Process	Technicolor
Colour Consultant	William Fritzsche
Editors	Milton Carruth, Al Clark
Art Directors	Alexander Golitzen, Emrich Nicholson
Set Designers	Russell A. Gausman, Oliver Emert
Music	Frank Skinner, Hans J. Salter, Joseph Gershenson
Choreography	Kenny Williams
Costumes	Bill Thomas
Technical Consultants	Rodolfo de Villeras (horses), Smokey Edwards (explosions), Dopey Dippleton (crowd movements), Al Ryatt

Jeff Chandler (*Marcianus*), Jack Palance (*Attila*), Ludmilla Tcherina (*Princess Pulcheria*), Rita Gam (*Kubra*), Jeff Morrow (*Paulinus*), George Dolenz (*Theodosius*), Eduard Franz (*Astrologer*), Allison Hayes (*Ildico*), Alexander Scourby (*Chrysaphius*), Sara Shane (*Myra*), Pat Hogan (*Sangiban*), Howard Petrie (*Gundahar*), Michael Ansara (*Edecon*), Leo Gordon (*Bleda*), Rusty Westcoatt (*Tula*), Chuck Roberson (*Mirrai*), Moroni Olsen (*Pope Leo*), Charles Horvath (*Olt*), Robo Bechi (*Chilothe*), Sim Iness (*Herculanus*), Walter Coy (*Valentinian*).

See p. 101 for description.

Filmed December 1953–February 1954. Released in USA, December 1954; GB, 10 January 1955. Running time, 92 min.
Distributors: Universal (USA), GFD (GB).

Captain Lightfoot (1954)

Production Company	Universal International
Producer	Ross Hunter
Director	Douglas Sirk
Assistant Director	John Sherwood
Script	W. R. Burnett, Oscar Brodney. Adapted from his own novel by W. R. Burnett
Director of Photography	Irving Glassberg (Cinemascope)
Colour Process	Technicolor
Colour Consultant	William Fritzsche
Editor	Frank Gross
Art Directors	Alexander Golitzen, Eric Orbom
Set Designers	Russell A. Gausman, Oliver Emert
Music	Joseph Gershenson
Costumes	Bill Thomas

Rock Hudson (*Michael Martin*), Barbara Rush (*Aga Doherty*), Jeff Morrow (*John Doherty* alias *Captain Thunderbolt*), Kathleen Ryan (*Lady Anne More*), Finlay Currie (*Callahan*), Denis O'Dea (*Regis*), Geoffrey Toone (*Captain Hood*), Shay Gorman (*Tim Keenan*), Robert

Bernal (*Clagett*), Nigel Fitzgerald (*Sir George Bracey*), Chris Casson (*Lord Clonmel*), Kenneth MacDonald (*High Steward*), James Devlin (*Tuer O'Brien*).

The Irish Revolution at the beginning of the nineteenth century. Michael Martin on the run is saved from the British Dragoons by the revolutionary leader John Doherty, disguised as a parson. After several mishaps, Martin comes to take Doherty's place, and is set to marry Doherty's daughter.

Filmed entirely on location in Ireland, June–August 1954. Released in USA, March 1955; GB, 9 May 1955. Running time, 91 min.
Distributors: Universal (USA), Rank (GB).

All That Heaven Allows (1955)

Production Company	Universal International
Producer	Ross Hunter
Production Manager	Sergei Petschnikoff
Director	Douglas Sirk
Assistant Directors	Joseph Kenny, George Lollier
Script	Peg Fenwick. From a story by Edna Lee and Harry Lee
Dialogue Director	Jack Daniels
Director of Photography	Russell Metty
Colour Process	Technicolor
Colour Consultant	William Fritzsche
Art Directors	Alexander Golitzen, Eric Orbom
Set Designers	Russell A. Gausman, Julia Heron
Music	Frank Skinner, Joseph Gershenson
Costumes	Bill Thomas

Jane Wyman (*Cary Scott*), Rock Hudson (*Ron Kirby*), Agnes Moorhead (*Sara Warren*), Conrad Nagel (*Harvey*), Virginia Grey (*Alida Anderson*), Gloria Talbott (*Kay Scott*), William Reynolds (*Ned Scott*), Jacqueline de Wit (*Mona Plash*), Charles Drake (*Mick Anderson*), Leigh Snowden (*Jo-Ann*), Merry Anders (*Mary Ann*), Donald Curtis (*Howard Hoffer*), Alex Gerry (*George Warren*).

A studio-chosen follow-up to *Magnificent Obsession*, with similar casting: Jane Wyman as the lonely widow in the small New England town; Agnes Moorhead as her best friend; Rock Hudson as the younger man. Jane Wyman falls in love with Hudson, a gardener. Her initial desire to flout the petit bourgeois pressures of her friends, and above all her two children, is gradually worn down. Only after 'nature' takes a hand and makes her so ill and miserable she can't go on, plus an accident, does she decide to go ahead.

Filmed January–February 1955. Released in USA, January 1956; GB, 26 September 1955. Running time, 89 min.
Distributors: Universal (USA), Rank (GB).

There's Always Tomorrow (1955)

Production Company	Universal International
Producer	Ross Hunter
Production Manager	Foster Thompson
Director	Douglas Sirk
Assistant Directors	Joseph E. Kenny, Gordon McLean

Script	Bernard C. Schoenfeld. Based on a story by Ursula Parrott
Dialogue Director	Jack Daniels
Director of Photography	Russell Metty
Editor	William Morgan
Art Directors	Alexander Golitzen, Eric Orbom
Set Designers	Russell A. Gausman, Julia Heron
Music	Herman Stein, Heinz Roemheld, Joseph Gershenson
Costumes	Jay Morley, Jr.

Barbara Stanwyck (*Norma Miller*), Fred MacMurray (*Clifford Groves*), Joan Bennett (*Marion Groves*), Pat Crowley (*Ann*), Jane Darwell (*Mrs Rogers*), William Reynolds (*Vincent Groves*), Gigi Perreau (*Ellen Groves*), Race Gentry (*Bob*), Myrna Hanson (*Ruth*), Judy Nugent (*Frankie Groves*), Helen Kleeb (*Mrs Walker*), Jane Howard (*Flower Girl*), Fred Nurney (*Tourist*), Dorothy Bruce (*Sales Manager*), Frances Mercer (*Ruth Doren*), Paul Smith (*Bellboy*), Sheila Bromley (*Woman from Pasadena*), Hermine Staler (*Tourist's Wife*), Hal Smith (*Bartender*), Ross Hunter.

Clifford Groves, a prosperous businessman, owner of a toy factory, is feeling neglected by his wife, Marion. He accidentally meets an old love, Norma Miller, and then again meets her accidentally at a desert resort, where he has gone without his wife, whom injury has kept at home. Groves' children take an active, moralistic part. Norma visits the home and then leaves. A re-make of Edward Sloman's *There's Always Tomorrow* (1934), with Frank Morgan, Binnie Barnes, Lois Wilson.

Filmed February–March 1955. Released in USA, February 1956; GB, 11 July 1956. Running time, 84 min.
Distributors: Universal (USA), Rank (GB).

1955 *Never Say Goodbye* (director, Jerry Hopper and [uncredited] Douglas Sirk; p.c., Universal International; script, Charles Hoffman from the script by Bruce Manning, John Klorer, and Leonard Lee, based on Pirandello's play *Come Prima, Meglio di Prima*). For Sirk's part in the film, see p. 108.

Written on the Wind (1956)

Production Company	Universal International
Producer	Albert Zugsmith
Production Manager	Norman Deming
Director	Douglas Sirk
Assistant Directors	William Holland, Wilson Shyer
Script	George Zuckerman. From the novel *Written on the Wind* by Robert Wilder
Director of Photography	Russell Metty
Colour Process	Technicolor
Colour Consultant	William Fritzsche
Editor	Russell F. Schoengarth
Special Effects	Clifford Stine
Art Directors	Alexander Golitzen, Robert Clatworthy
Set Designers	Russell A. Gausman, Julia Heron
Music	Frank Skinner
Musical Supervisor	Joseph Gershenson
Lyric:	
'Written on the Wind'	by Victor Young and Sammy Cahn, sung by The Four Aces
Costumes	Bill Thomas, Jay Morley, Jr

Rock Hudson (*Mitch Wayne*), Lauren Bacall (*Lucy Hadley*), Robert Stack (*Kyle Hadley*), Dorothy Malone (*Marylee Hadley*), Robert Keith (*Jasper Hadley*), Grant Williams (*Biff Miley*), Harry Shannon (*Hoak Wayne*), Robert J. Wilke (*Dan Willis*), Edward C. Platt (*Dr Cochrane*), John Larch (*Roy Carter*), Joseph Cranby (*R. J. Courtney*), Roy Glenn (*Sam*), Maide Norman (*Bertha*).

Shot mainly in a flashback. A rich and neurotic alcoholic Texas oilman, Kyle Hadley, marries a designer, Lucy Hadley. His sister Marylee is passionately in love with his aide, Mitch Wayne. After about a year of marriage, Hadley begins to worry about his wife not being pregnant. He starts drinking again. Wayne comes under suspicion when Lucy announces she is going to have a child. Hadley is killed in a fight 'by accident'. After a trial (cf. *Schlussakkord*), at which all hangs on Marylee's testimony, Wayne is acquitted.

Filmed November 1955–January 1956. Released in USA, January 1957; GB, 29 October 1956. Running time, 92 min.
Distributors: Universal (USA), Rank (GB).

Dorothy Malone received an Academy Award as best supporting actress.

Battle Hymn (1956)

Production Company	Universal International
Producer	Ross Hunter
Production Manager	Norman Deming
Director	Douglas Sirk
Second Unit	James C. Havens
Assistant Directors	Marshall Green, Terry Nelson
Script	Charles Grayson, Vincent B. Evans. Based on the true story of Colonel Dean Hess, later written into a book entitled *Battle Hymn*
Director of Photography	Russell Metty (Cinemascope)
Colour Process	Technicolor
Special Effects	Clifford Stine
Editor	Russell F. Schoengarth
Art Directors	Alexander Golitzen, Emrich Nicholson
Set Designers	Russell A. Gausman, Oliver Emert
Music	Frank Skinner, Joseph Gershenson
Costumes	Bill Thomas
Technical Consultant	Colonel Dean Hess

Rock Hudson (*Colonel Dean Hess*), Anna Kashfi (*En Soon Yang*), Dan Duryea (*Sergeant Herman*), Don de Fore (*Captain Skidmore*), Martha Hyer (*Mary Hess*), Jock Mahoney (*Commander Moore*), Alan Hale (*Mess Sergeant*), James Edwards (*Lieutenant Maples*), Philip Ahn (*Old Man*), Carl Benton Reid (*Deacon Edwards*), 25 children from 'The Orphans Home of Korea' as themselves. The film is presented by General Earle C. Partridge who commanded the 5th Air Force in Korea (see p. 113).

The story of an American airman, 'Killer' Hess. See p. 110.

Filmed March–May 1956. Released in USA, March 1957; GB, 25 February 1957. Running time, 108 min.
Distributors: Universal (USA), Rank (GB).

Interlude (1956)

Production Company	Universal International
Producer	Ross Hunter
Production Manager	Norman Deming
Director	Douglas Sirk
Assistant Director	Marshall Green
Script	Daniel Fuchs, Franklin Coon. Adapted by Inez Cocke from the scenario by Dwight Taylor, loosely derived from the novel *Serenade* by James Cain
Director of Photography	William Daniels (Cinemascope)
Colour Process	Technicolor
Colour Consultant	William Fritzsche
Editor	Russell F. Schoengarth
Art Directors	Alexander Golitzen, Robert E. Smith
Set Designer	Russell A. Gausman
Music	Frank Skinner, Joseph Gershenson; themes from Beethoven, Mozart, Wagner, Brahms, Liszt, and Schumann
Lyric:	
'Interlude'	Paul Francis Webster, Frank Skinner; sung by the McGuire Sisters
Costumes	Jay A. Morley, Jr
Technical Consultant	Wolfgang Edward Rebner

June Allyson (*Helen Banning*), Rossano Brazzi (*Tonio Fischer*), Marianne Cook (*Reni Fischer*), Françoise Rosay (*Countess Reinhart*), Keith Andes (*Dr Morley Dwyer*), Frances Bergen (*Gertrude Kirk*), Jane Wyatt (*Prue Stubbins*), Lisa Heling (*Housekeeper*), Herman Schwedt (*Henig*), Anthony Tripoli (*Dr Smith*), John Stein (*Dr Stein*).

An American girl, Helen Banning, comes to Munich to get away. There she meets a rich conductor, Tonio Fischer. They fall in love after a picnic and a spectacular thunderstorm. Fischer is meanwhile concealing a broken-down wife, Reni, while Helen is being diligently and pathetically pursued by a young American doctor, Morley Dwyer. After Reni Fischer's attempted suicide, Helen decides to return to her 'real home' – America – with the doctor. For the source of the story, see p. 113. Sirk shot from a script itself derived from Dwight Taylor's loose adaptation of James Cain's *Serenade* for John Stahl's *When Tomorrow Comes* (1939, with Charles Boyer and Irene Dunne). *Serenade* (d. Anthony Mann, 1956) is also based indirectly on the same novel. Sirk's film was 're-made' in 1967, as *Interlude* (d. Kevin Billington).

Filmed on location in Bavaria and Salzburg, Austria. Released in USA, September 1957; GB, 29 July 1957. Running time, 90 min.
Distributors: Universal (USA), Rank (GB).

The Tarnished Angels (1957)

Production Company	Universal International
Producer	Albert Zugsmith
Production Manager	Tom Shaw
Director	Douglas Sirk
Assistant Director	David Silver
Script	George Zuckerman. From the novel *Pylon* by William Faulkner
Director of Photography	Irving Glassberg (Cinemascope)
Special Effects	Clifford Stine

Editor	Russell F. Schoengarth
Art Directors	Alexander Golitzen, Alfred Sweeney
Set Designers	Russell A. Gausman, Oliver Emert
Music	Frank Skinner, Joseph Gershenson
Costumes	Bill Thomas

Rock Hudson (*Burke Devlin*), Robert Stack (*Roger Shumann*), Dorothy Malone (*Laverne Shumann*), Jack Carson (*Jiggs*), Robert Middleton (*Matt Ord*), Alan Reed (*Colonel Fineman*), Alexander Lockwood (*Sam Hagood*), Chris Olsen (*Jack Shumann*), Robert J. Wilke (*Hank*), Troy Donahue (*Frank Burnham*).

The Depression: a hard-drinking New Orleans reporter, Burke Devlin, becomes obsessed with a 'family' of flyers: the pilot Roger Shumann, the parachute jumper Laverne, the mechanic Jiggs, and their son. Laverne is woman as object: object to be stared at jumping, merchandise to be sold to Matt Ord to obtain a plane, just as she was 'acquired' by rolling dice. The theme of flying, set off against the insecurity of life on the ground (cf. *Written on the Wind, Battle Hymn*) at its most explicit – and then masterfully turned by Shumann's suicide. 'While I was still at Leipzig I wrote a novelette based on *Pylon*, and I even thought of trying to stage it for a while, but I wasn't satisfied with it. Then I took it to Ufa, but they weren't interested in a flying picture' (Sirk).

Outstandingly the best adaptation to the screen of any Faulkner story, acknowledged as such by Faulkner himself. It is perhaps worth insisting on this in view of the widespread myths about 'adaptations' and Faulkner adaptations in particular.

Filmed at San Diego December 1956–February 1957. Released in USA, January 1958; GB, 30 December 1957. Running time, 91 min.
Distributors: Universal (USA), Rank (GB).

A Time to Love and a Time to Die (1957)

Production Company	Universal International
Producer	Robert Arthur
Production Manager	Norman W. Deming
Assistant Production Manager	Henz Gotze
Director	Douglas Sirk
Assistant Directors	Joseph E. Kenny, Dr Michael Braun
Script	Orin Jannings. From the novel by Erich Maria Remarque
Director of Photography	Russell Metty (Cinemascope)
Colour Process	Eastmancolor
Special Effects	Clifford Stine, 'Whitey' McMahan
Editor	Ted J. Kent
Art Directors	Alexander Golitzen, Alfred Sweeney
Set Designers	Russell A. Gausman
Music	Miklos Rozsa
Costumes	Bill Thomas
Technical Consultant	Captain Herman Ulbricht

John Gavin (*Ernst Graeber*), Lilo Pulver (*Elizabeth Kruse*), Jock Mahony (*Immerman*), Don De Fore (*Boettcher*), Keenan Wynn (*Reuter*), Erich Maria Remarque (*Professor Pohlmann*), Dieter Borsche (*Captain Rahe*), Barbara Rutting (*Woman Guerilla*), Thayer David (*Oscar Binding*), Charles Regnier (*Josef*), Dorothea Wieck (*Frau Lieser*), Alexander Engel (*Mad Air-raid Warden*), Karl Ludwig Lindt (*Dr Karl Fressenburg*), Agnes Windeck (*Frau Witte*), Alice Treff (*Frau Langer*), Klaus Kinski (*Gestapo Lieutenant*), Kurt Meisel (*Heini*).

170

A young German soldier, Ernst Graeber, gets leave during the German retreat from Russia. Back home he meets and falls in love with a girl, Elizabeth Kruse. They marry. Bombed from house to house, from restaurant to cellar, the lovers live amid a landscape of ruins, actual and incipient. After a beautiful elliptic departure (Ernst leaving is filmed as another soldier is saying goodbye to his wife and child), Ernst is killed after turning against his superiors and liberating some Soviet partisans.

'I have never believed in Germany at war so much as watching this American film made in time of peace' (Godard).

Filmed entirely on location in Germany, August–December 1957. Released in USA, July 1958; GB, 8 September 1958. Running time, 133 min.

Distributors: Universal (USA), Rank (GB).

Not to be confused with *A Time to Live and a Time to Die* (Louis Malle's *Le Feu Follet*).

Imitation of Life (1958)

Production Company	Universal International
Producer	Ross Hunter
Director	Douglas Sirk
Assistant Directors	Frank Shaw, Wilson Shyer
Script	Eleanore Griffin, Allan Scott. From the novel by Fannie Hurst
Director of Photography	Russell Metty
Colour Process	Eastmancolor
Special Effects	Clifford Stine
Editor	Milton Carruth
Art Directors	Alexander Golitzen, Richard H. Reidel
Set Designers	Russell A. Gausman, Julia Heron
Music	Frank Skinner
Lyrics:	
'Imitation of Life'	Paul Francis Webster, Sammy Fain; sung by Earl Grant
'Empty Arms'	Frederick Herbert, Arnold Hughes; sung by Susan Kohner
'Trouble of the World'	sung by Mahalia Jackson
Costumes	Bill Thomas
Gowns	Jean Louis (for Lana Turner)

Lana Turner (*Lora Meredith*), John Gavin (*Steve Archer*), Sandra Dee (*Susie Meredith at 16*), Terry Burnham (*Susie at 6*), Susan Kohner (*Sarah Jane Johnson at 18*), Karen Dicker (*Sarah Jane at 8*), Juanita Moore (*Annie Johnson*), Dan O'Herlihy (*David Edwards*), Robert Alda (*Allen Loomis*), Troy Donahue (*Frankie*), Maida Severn (*Teacher*), Mahalia Jackson as herself.

A down-and-out actress, Lora Meredith, with a small daughter hires a down-and-out black woman with a small daughter to be her maid and servant. She decides to try and press on with her career, at the expense of her daughter – and of her lover, Steve Archer, who gives up and marries someone else. Sarah Jane, in an impossible position as daughter of the maid and 'friend' of Lora's daughter Susie, tries to pass as white. She is beaten up by Frankie in an alleyway, has recurrent painful rows with her mother, attempts to demonstrate her slave condition serving cocktails to Lora Meredith and a visiting Italian movie director, and finally goes off to work in night clubs. The entire end of the film is a long and moving contemplation of Sarah Jane's attempts at living in the world of white show-business, culminating with her mother's grandiose funeral. One may note that Lora's first stage success in the film is titled *Stopover*; her other hits mostly have titles involving the word 'laughter'.

Sirk's goodbye to America and to films. A 're-make' of John Stahl's *Imitation of Life* (1934), with Claudette Colbert and Warren Williams.

Filmed August–October, 1958. Released in USA, April 1959; GB, 11 May 1959. Running time, 125 min.
Distributors: Universal (USA), Rank (GB). Current GB distributor: Columbia (16 mm.)
After *Imitation of Life*, Sirk terminated his contract with Universal.

Film Projects (1959–64)

c. 1959 *The Streets of Montmartre:* a project on Utrillo and Suzanne Valadon. Screenplay by Ionesco and Sirk. Louis Jourdan was projected in the lead. Abandoned because of Sirk's illness.

c. 1959. *The Dark at the Top of the Stairs:* project offered by Jack Warner, after Sirk had broken with Universal. Sirk declined. It was made in 1960 by Delbert Mann.

1959 *Arena:* based on the novel *Arena* by Charles Grayson. 'I think it was probably after *Imitation of Life*, there was a project to try and make a picture out of *Arena*. Charlie Grayson had worked with me on *Battle Hymn*, and he came over to Switzerland, and I think we worked on it about five weeks or so' (Sirk).

c. 1961. *Madame X:* a Ross Hunter project, based on the play *Madame X* by Alexandre Bisson. Lana Turner was envisaged for the lead part. 'Just the sort of thing I did not want to go on doing' (Sirk). (He had staged the play at Chemnitz in 1922–23, see p. 17.) Eventually made by David Lowell Rich, with Lana Turner, in 1966.

1962 *The Magic Mountain:* Sirk was approached by Richard Schweizer, a friend of Thomas Mann, about making a film out of the novel. Erika Mann, Thomas Mann's daughter, had been an actress in Sirk's theatre in Bremen in the mid-1920s, and wanted to work on the script. Sirk appears to have discussed it as a vague possibility with Thomas Mann much earlier. 'Like the other things, it needed to be completely transformed. It had good characters in it ... it might have been possible. But I'm not sure the social criticism would stand up. I would have had to do it as a costume picture. Times had changed' (Sirk).

1963 *Confessions of an Opium Eater:* Sirk had suggested this as a project to Zugsmith earlier, but it had not come to fruition. Zugsmith shot it himself in 1963, with Vincent Price in the lead. Alternatively known as *Evils of Chinatown* or *Souls for Sale*. An underground masterpiece. Based on Thomas de Quincey's *Confessions of an English Opium Eater*.

1964 *Fanny Hill:* Zugsmith wanted Sirk to direct this. Sirk, now in definitive retirement from films, declined. Directed by Zugsmith. Based on the novel by John Cleland.

Theatre (1963–69)

Sirk, under his earlier name of Detlef Sierck, staged the following plays in Germany after his retirement from Hollywood:

1963 *Cyrano de Bergerac* (Edmond Rostand). Residenztheater, Munich.

1964 *Le Roi Se Meurt* (Ionesco), Residenztheater, Munich.

1965 *The Tempest* (Shakespeare), Residenztheater, Munich.

1966 *Der Parasit* (Schiller), Residenztheater, Munich.

1967 *L'Avare* (Molière), Residenztheater, Munich.

1969 *The Seven Descents of Myrtle* (Tennessee Williams), Thalia Theater, Hamburg.

Bibliography

There is no adequate study of Sirk in any language. Brief essays on his work are to be found in Andrew Sarris, *The American Cinema*, New York, 1968; Jean-Pierre Coursodon and Bertrand Tavernier, *Trente Ans de Cinéma Americain*, Paris, 1970; *Cahiers du Cinéma*, No. 189, April 1967 (Jean-Louis Comolli); Raymond Bellour and Jean-Jacques Brochier, *Dictionnaire du Cinéma*, Paris, 1966: all these are appreciative, but rather short. Most of the biofilmographies in film dictionaries are inaccurate or of little value. *Screen*, Vol. 12, No. 2 (Summer 1971), is a special issue devoted largely to Sirk.

For Sirk's theatre work in Germany, the main source is *33 Jahre Bremer Schauspielhaus im Spiegel der Zeitkritik*, Bremen, n.d. (Carl Schünemann Verlag): this deals only with Sirk's work in Bremen (1923–29). Those interested in wider events can consult: on the Bavarian Soviet, Ernst Toller *I Was a German*, London, 1934, a most readable, if somewhat unilateral account; Allan Mitchell, *Revolution in Bavaria 1918–1919*, Princeton, NJ, 1965, is useful but mainly about Eisner; on the general cultural situation in Germany between the end of the First World War and 1933, Peter Gay, *Weimar Culture*, London, 1969, is a slim guide to a dense epoch; some of the contemporary plays which Sirk staged (and their authors) are dealt with in H. F. Garten, *Modern German Drama*, London, 1959; Günther Rühle, *Theater für die Republik 1917–1933*, Frankfurt am Main, 1967, is an extremely careful and well-annotated source. Several of the people Sirk mentions in the text have written autobiographies or memoirs: notable among these are Arnolt Bronnen, *Gibt zum Protokoll*, Hamburg, 1954, and Carl Zuckmayer, *Als Wär's ein Stück von mir*, Vienna, 1966.

Much the best source in English on the German cinema under the Hitler regime is David Stewart Hull, *Film in the Third Reich*, Berkeley and Los Angeles, 1969 (which discusses some of Sirk's German films and evokes the working conditions extremely well); Joseph Wulf, *Theater und Film im Dritten Reich*, Gütersloh, 1964 (now Rowohlt paperback) has some useful information; on Ufa, see H. P. Manz, *Ufa und der Frühe Deutsche Film*, Zurich, 1963. Zarah Leander, star of Sirk's last two German films, has written an autobiography, *Vill Ni Se En Diva?*, Stockholm, 1958, which has a whole chapter on *Zu Neuen Ufern*, but fails to mention Sirk.

A number of people who worked with Sirk in America have also written memoirs: George Sanders, *Memoirs of a Professional Cad*, London, 1960, is a witty but elliptical account of his life by the actor who played the lead in Sirk's first American films; the picture is fleshed out by Zsa Zsa Gabor in *Zsa Zsa Gabor* by Gerold Frank, London, 1960. Sterling Hayden (*Take Me to Town*) has written a striking and moving autobiography, *Wanderer*, London, 1964. William Daniels, who was cameraman on four of Sirk's American films, talks about his work in Charles Higham, *Hollywood Cameramen*, London and Bloomington, Indiana, 1970. Hanns Eisler, who worked on *Scandal in Paris*, is author of *Composing for the Films*, London, 1951.

173

Reviews of individual films

Summer Storm, James Agee in *On Film*, London, 1967; *The First Legion*, Dave Grosz, *Screen*, Summer 1971; *Taza, Son of Cochise*, Patrick Brion, *Le Western*, ed. *Artsept*, Paris, 1966; *Magnificent Obsession*, Phillippe Demonsablon, *Cahiers du Cinéma* 49 (July 1955); *Written on the Wind*, Louis Marcorelles, *Cahiers du Cinéma* 69 (March 1957); *The Tarnished Angels*, Kingsley Canham, *Films and Filming*, January 1970 – Luc Moullet, *Cahiers du Cinéma* 87 (September 1958) – Fred Camper, *Screen*, Summer 1971 – Pauline Kael in *Kiss Kiss, Bang Bang*, London, 1970; *A Time to Love and a Time to Die*, Philippe Haudiquet, *Image et Son*, 176–7 (September–October 1964) – Jean-Luc Godard, *Cahiers du Cinéma* 94 (April 1959) and now in the special issue of *Screen* on Sirk, 1971; *All That Heaven Allows* and *A Time to Love and a Time to Die* (joint review), Paul Joannides, *Cinema* (Cambridge–London, UK), No. 5–6 (August 1970); *Imitation of Life*, Jean-Jacques Camelin, *Image et Son* 189 (December 1965) – Luc Moullet, *Cahiers du Cinéma* 104 (February 1960) – R. W. Fassbinder, *Fernsehen und Film*, February 1971.

A dossier of Sirk's work in both theatre and film has been assembled, and copies are located in the British and American Film Institute Libraries. I should be very glad to hear from anybody doing research on Sirk, and in particular who knows of prints of his early shorts, of either version of *April, April*, of *Hofkonzert* and *Accord Final*.

174

The loneliness of the New England widow at Christmastime: Jane Wyman in *All That Heaven Allows*

Acknowledgements

I have been enormously aided in the production of this book by many people – more than I can thank by name here. I am especially grateful to Jim Kitses, formerly of the American Film Institute for first agreeing to take on the project of an Oral History on Douglas Sirk; to Gail Naughton, Christopher Williams, and Peter Wollen of the British Film Institute for much assistance in preparing the book; to the W. F. Murnau-Stiftung, Wiesbaden, for screening four of Sirk's early films for me; to the Deutsches Institut für Filmkunde, Wiesbaden, for their help in researching material on Sirk's German films, and the use of an excellent library; to the Stichting Nederlands Filmmuseum, Amsterdam, for providing information and stills on Sirk's Dutch films; to Rudolph Joseph of the Filmmuseum, Munich, for helping me track down the German films; to Iri Seiser of the Residenztheater, Munich, for information on Sirk's later theatre work in Munich; to Richard Hamilton, Erna and Curt Burgauer, and the Tate Gallery for permission to reproduce the painting on p. 80, and to quote from Richard Hamilton's writings; to the Neue Pinakothek, Munich, for permission to reproduce the painting on p. 20; to Faber & Faber (London) and Harcourt Brace Jovanovich (New York) for the quotations from 'The Love Song of J. Alfred Prufrock' and 'The Waste Land', from *Collected Poems 1909–1962* by T. S. Eliot; to Calder & Boyars for the quotation from Edward Bond's play *Early Morning*, London, 1968; in preparing the filmography I would like to thank Laura Wollen, and also Patrick Brion and Dominique Rabourdin, who assembled the first filmography in *Cahiers du Cinéma*, on which I have relied heavily.

Fred Camper of M.I.T. and Sam Rohdie generously made available unpublished manuscripts on Sirk. Thomas Elsaesser was of invaluable aid in orienting the original research on Sirk's theatre work in Germany. And I am more than grateful to many friends, including Ben Brewster, Cloe Peploe, Rosamond Lomax, and Goffredo Fofi for their stimulating interest in the project, and the many insights they gave me. Lastly, I would like to acknowledge the great hospitality of Adriana Vanini, and the Campi at Muzzano.

Stills by courtesy of: Douglas Sirk, Albert Zugsmith; Columbia, Deutsches Institut für Filmkunde, M-G-M, Nederlands Filmmuseum, UFA-International, United Artists, Universal (Philip Gerard), and the Stills Library of the National Film Archive.